"Do you think I don't feel guilty—loving you?"

Dev spoke with helpless frustration.

"I'm sure it's been a terrible experience," Alicia said contemptuously. "But your ordeal is through. I want you to go."

"Alicia, will you give me a chance?" he exclaimed, catching her wrist.

"I've given you enough," she said with cutting scorn, and he dropped his hand. "You were rather kind, and you certainly taught me a lot. But I'm not that pathetic, clinging little fool any longer, and I don't need your *services.* I think I've paid an awfully high price for them as it is."

He was very pale. "Listen to me—"he said urgently.

"I never want to hear or see you again," she ground out fiercely. "Get out of my house!"

WELCOME
TO THE WONDERFUL WORLD
OF *Harlequin Romances*

Interesting, informative and entertaining,
each Harlequin Romance portrays an appealing
and original love story. With a varied array
of settings, we may lure you on an African safari,
to a quaint Welsh village, or an exotic Riviera
location—anywhere and everywhere that adventurous
men and women fall in love.

As publishers of Harlequin Romances, we're
extremely proud of our books. Since 1949,
Harlequin Enterprises has built its publishing
reputation on the solid base of quality and
originality. Our stories are the most popular
paperback romances sold in North America; every
month, six new titles are released and sold at
nearly every book-selling store in Canada and the
United States.

For a list of all titles currently available,
send your name and address to:

HARLEQUIN READER SERVICE,
(In the U.S.) P.O. Box 52040, Phoenix, AZ 85072-2040
(In Canada) P.O. Box 2800, Postal Station A
5170 Yonge Street, Willowdale, Ont. M2N 6J3

We sincerely hope you enjoy reading
this Harlequin Romance.

Yours truly,

THE PUBLISHERS
Harlequin Romances

Love's Good Fortune

Louise Harris

Harlequin Books

TORONTO · NEW YORK · LONDON
AMSTERDAM · PARIS · SYDNEY · HAMBURG
STOCKHOLM · ATHENS · TOKYO · MILAN

Original hardcover edition published in 1984
by Mills & Boon Limited

ISBN 0-373-02685-4

Harlequin Romance first edition April 1985

CHAPTER ONE

THE first time Alicia saw Devereaux Lloyd Rafferty was at a party. One of those artists' parties Aunt Elizabeth so disapproved of—they called them 'bohemian' in her day—crowded, noisy and wild. Not an actual orgy, but certainly not what Alicia had been brought up on—which was just as well, in her opinion.

Afterwards, there wasn't much Alicia remembered about the evening: not where the party was held, nor who had actually brought her, nor even who was there. The music was loud and raw, and the wriggling couples dancing in the haze of smoke and hanging plants, looked like something from a *film noir*. All in all it was pretty routine. Then Alicia had looked out across the mass of familiar strangers and seen him.

'Who's that?' she asked her companion. He was someone she knew slightly from one of her art classes and she interrupted his half-hearted attempt to seduce her, or rather the Carrington millions, into going home with him. She couldn't remember his name, which made them about equal, as all he remembered about her *was* her name.

'Who?' He followed her line of perception to where the man stood, leaning nonchalantly against a fireplace painted on the far wall. He was listening to a small, thin girl with cropped black hair and a sarcastic face, his restless eyes moving over the crowd, his expression one of cynical amusement.

'Don't you know?' Her companion was honestly amazed. 'That's Dev Rafferty.'

Devereaux Rafferty? No wonder her fellow art student was surprised. Who, if they knew anything about art at all, did not know of Dev Rafferty? His brilliant innovative work had sent Art spinning in a new direction. He defied Modern Art theory and criticism at every turn, preferring to 'do art rather than talk it.' The critics hated and adored him. He wouldn't play the game. He wouldn't revile the old masters or discuss the new trends. He was an absolute genius and they forgave him his eccentricities. Alicia knew quite a bit about Dev Rafferty, but she had never seen him before. She was interested.

He didn't look at all as she had imagined. She wasn't disappointed, but she was surprised. She had expected someone big, powerful and flamboyant. Rafferty was tall and gracefully built, like a dancer. His hair was chestnut and wavy, his skin fair. He had a classically perfect profile: fine bones, high, hollowed cheeks. A clever face, almost a beautiful face. And yes, a forceful, dynamic personality, but not flamboyant. Rather highly strung, like a thorough-bred.

'Would you like to be introduced?' Alicia's companion asked maliciously. That was to pay her back for not being impressed with *him*. After all, he was very good-looking and knew it, and he had been spending a lot of time and charm on this plain, shy, *boring* girl who—merely because she was filthy rich—had the nerve to snub him.

'Yes, I would,' Alicia replied simply to his evident surprise, and he led her through the jungle of people to the far wall where Dev Rafferty and his companion stood.

'Dev, here's a great admirer of yours,' Alicia's companion said sardonically, nudging her forward. Alicia was a tall girl, and her eyes met Rafferty's almost on a level. They were green, she noticed, and tilted up at the corners giving his face a strange, almost elfin look.

'Alicia *Carrington*,' Alicia's companion stressed. 'God's gift to art, but not as an artist.'

'Certainly not as a model,' Rafferty's companion put in coolly. This was delivered with an indifferent callousness that was almost shocking. Alicia looked down more disbelieving than anything into a pair of lovely violet eyes and a beautiful, arrogant face. The woman's brows arched challengingly and quick colour rushed into Alicia's cheeks.

'I don't know,' Rafferty said consideringly. He had a lazy, drawling voice. 'It's a face I'd love to paint.' He smiled at Alicia. He had a devastating smile. 'Beautiful bones and lots of character.'

He did not look like a kind man, nor one to suffer fools, but his kindness had been real and automatic. That was what impressed Alicia: his instinctive, casual parrying of meanness. He probably didn't think about it twice, and five minutes later he had left the party with his viper-tongued beauty, but he was all Alicia remembered of the night.

Alicia was an early riser. Weekdays, an early morning was necessary because of class. Weekends, the previous night's entertainment not withstanding, she rose early to exercise her horse. She liked the peace and quiet of the morning before her aunt rose. As a young girl, morning had usually offered Alicia her only solitude and respite.

This morning, however, her sister Jacqueline, who

was staying the weekend, was already breakfasting by the time Alicia reached the dining room. Alicia quashed a momentary flicker of disappointment. She had looked forward to a leisurely breakfast, mulling over last night's party. But since Jacqueline had married Victor, Alicia hadn't seen much of her sister, and she supposed it was churlish to resent her bad timing.

'Good morning!' Jacqueline remarked, looking up as Alicia dropped into the chair opposite. Her tone was faintly dry. 'I'm surprised to see you up so early. What time did you finally get in last night?'

Since Jacqueline probably knew what time Alicia arrived home, she wondered why her sister bothered to ask? She shrugged noncommittally, reaching for the coffee pot.

'Quite the little night-owl, aren't we?' Jacqueline was watching her with cool consideration, making Alicia feel self-conscious and defensive. Although Jacqueline was only a few years older, she always intimidated Alicia with her cool poise and ready sarcasm.

'What do you mean?' Alicia asked awkwardly, pouring herself a half-cup of coffee. She didn't care for coffee, but Aunt Elizabeth did, and that was all that was served at Carrington House.

'I mean,' Jacqueline said briskly, 'things have changed since I left home.'

Alicia shrugged. Her rather sulky silence and air of slouching defensiveness never failed to irritate Jacqueline who, after a brief pause, cracked open her hardboiled egg with a punitive sharpness. Alicia eyed her sister cautiously.

Jacqueline was the beauty of the family. She had inherited their mother's looks: the black hair and

blue eyes, the sharp, aristocratic bones of the Severs-
ly side. Alicia also had blue eyes, but they were
an ordinary blue and not the rare milky-blue of
Jacqueline's. Alicia's hair was mousy-brown
and she didn't bother with the frequent expensive cuts and treatments Jacqueline indulged in.
Alicia's hair was very long, almost to her waist,
and unreasonably a point of irritation with her
family.

Alert to Alicia's nervous brushing of some long,
lank strands behind her ear, Jacqueline said in a
suddenly annoyed voice, '*Why* don't you get that
cut?'

'I like it,' Alicia replied mildly. Her sister eyed her
in exasperation. They had been raised alike, in the
same house by the same Aunt Elizabeth, but they
might easily have been strangers. Alicia was fond of
Jacqueline and supposed her sister was fond of her,
but they had never been friends.

Jacqueline said rather wearily, 'You know, it's one
thing to go through this adolescent rebellion non-
sense when you're an adolescent, but you're twenty-
three now. I was married at your age.'

'So?'

'*So?* So it's time to start acting like a woman of your
age. What is this idea of a degree?'

'I've been going to school for years,' Alicia pointed
out.

'Yes, but my God! Nobody took that seriously. But
now—'

Now what, Alicia wondered warily. Now that it
looked like she would graduate?

'On its own, an education wouldn't be a bad
thing,' Jacqueline was continuing reasonably, 'but
when you put it together with all the rest: the way

you dress, for instance, your social life—you rarely date—and these parties where heaven knows what goes on—drugs, sex . . .'

Alicia looked up with a faint, quizzical gleam of humour at the mounting sense of scandal in her sister's tone, but all humour died from her face as Jacqueline finished:

'Aunt Elizabeth is very worried about you.'

'She needn't be,' Alicia muttered, toying with her spoon.

'How can she help but be? She thinks she's failed you somehow. Why else would you . . . reject your family and name?'

'I don't reject them!' Against her will, Alicia's voice shot up agitatedly.

'Don't you?' Jacqueline's milky-blue eyes studied Alicia's flushed face grimly. 'Do you honestly think a *Carrington* should drag her name through every little murky club, down every sordid street and into every seedy party in London? Is that how you were brought up?'

'It's not like that!' Alicia cried. 'I don't *drag* my name anywhere. I don't do anything to disgrace the *noble* name of Carrington. These people are fun— some of them—and talented too. More fun than the stuffed shirts *you* run with.' She stopped, shocked at herself, but Jacqueline was unscathed.

'And I'll bet you just fit right in with these wildly talented people?' Her smile was derisive. Under her ironic eye Alicia's colour mounted.

'They barely notice me,' Alicia delivered.

'Terrific! You're the fly on the wall getting her vicarious thrills by watching the other half live!'

Alicia was too hurt to answer this sensibly, beyond a glare across the table. Besides, she knew that her sister and Aunt Elizabeth wanted what was best for her—as they saw it.

Alicia had had plenty of time to dwell on the differences between her sister and herself. She had given plenty of thought to what it was about her that left her family bewildered and frustrated. She had reached the conclusion that Aunt Elizabeth had known how to deal with Jacqueline because Jacqueline's nature was similar to her own. But Alicia, impulsive and painfully sensitive, had left her aunt feeling inadequate. It simply was not in her to give her dead brother's child the vast amount of reassurance and affection she needed. Alicia did not resent her aunt for her inability, and she was not jealous, really, of Jacqueline. Somewhere, she knew, there were people like herself—at least one other person. She wanted to find that someone. She needed to communicate, to share the things she felt and thought; things incomprehensible to her aunt and sister. Alicia knew she would never find anyone like that in the vast social circle the Carringtons belonged to. But you couldn't try and explain ideas like that to Jacqueline, who, at best, would be appalled at the alternative.

And after all, there was no guarantee she would find what she was looking for at parties like the one last night. That party was more interesting than the ones she had grown up attending, but Alicia admitted honestly that she probably thought so only because it was all still new to her. Wealthy or poor, people were much the same all over: small-minded and inflexible—even in their 'free' attitudes.

Not all of them.

Alicia thought of Dev Rafferty with a sudden quivering excitement in her stomach. *He* was diferent. Unlike anyone she knew. She remembered his off-handed verbal rescue with a quick rush of warmth. It seemed especially kind because she was terrible at verbal encounters. She had been completely unprepared for the impersonal vindictiveness of the other woman. What a terrible person, she thought uneasily, although very beautiful. Dev Rafferty had looked like someone able to hold his own in any scrap.

You wouldn't meet anyone like Dev Rafferty in Jacqueline's crowd. There was nothing smug or pompous about him. None of that beefy, well-fed mentality so typical of Victor, Jacqueline's husband. Alicia still couldn't believe Jacqueline had married Victor—he was so dull and heavy. Everything about him was heavy: his looks, his humour, the way his mind moved. How could Jacqueline love someone like that? Because he had money and position and the name 'Smith-Lawes'? When Alicia imagined someone like Victor making love to her she felt physically sick. Not for all the power and prestige in the world—it was almost like being a prostitute. She would rather spend her entire life alone than share it with someone she detested.

But maybe, Alicia thought with a surreptitious peek at her sister, Jacqueline really loved Victor? It didn't seem possible, but then she supposed most of the things she did didn't seem possible to Jacqueline, either. Jacqueline couldn't see the point of getting a University degree. Alicia would never have to work, why struggle through years of study and effort? Jacqueline couldn't see why Alicia wanted a flat of her own—the current family argument. She thought Alicia was a little paranoid about her privacy. Further, she didn't understand why Alicia wouldn't go out with the personable young men of good family who asked her. How did Alicia know she didn't like a man until she'd spent some time with him?

It was no use arguing, Alicia knew. Aunt Elizabeth and Jacqueline were never going to see life her way—and she would rather be buried alive than live their way. Aunt Elizabeth and Jacqueline thought she was sullen because she wouldn't argue—or agree—with them over her future. Alicia didn't see any point in quarrelling, which she hated, and she didn't see any point in rehashing the same old subject. She didn't want to hurt them—any more than they did her—but she refused to sacrifice her life to the Carrington image. So she said now, placatingly;

'I'd never do anything to hurt Aunt Elizabeth—or you.'

'You would be hurting yourself as well,' Jacqeuline pointed out bluntly. Jacqueline was talking 'prospects'.

'I know that.'

'I hope so.' Jacqueline's unspoken doubt hung like a cloud over the breakfast table. Alicia choked down her cereal as quickly as possible, excused herself and fled to the stable.

In the familiar warmth of the stable, Alicia could drop her guard and give way to her anxieties. One didn't have to put on a brave face with a horse. A horse didn't hold a grudge if you disappointed its ambitions. She could feel the direction the wind blew. Things were shaping up for a family 'scene'. There hadn't been one in years, even her decision to start University had slipped by with only a few scathing remarks. But trouble was in the air. Her student lifestyle was about to come under public censure, probably initiated by her desire to move out. The last scene had been over the same subject, and she had been foiled then—as she would probably be foiled now—by the fact that Aunt Elizabeth held the purse strings. Until she graduated, and could find a job, she was trapped.

Trapped. Aunt Elizabeth would find that choice of word melodramatic, but trapped she was, Alicia thought dispiritedly, saddling up her bay jumper. Call it what she would, she was twenty-three years old and, barring miracles, she could look forward to another two years of prisondom.

She gritted her jaw, cinching up the saddle girth. Regardless of what her family said or did, there was no stopping her for ever. She would just keep on as she had been, quietly, stubbornly pursuing her own goals. As long as she didn't give in or give up, one of these days she would be free. *Free.* Another melodramatic word, no doubt. Alicia shrugged and swung up into the saddle, guiding her horse through the training gate and nudging him towards the first jump.

'Hey, Carrington!'

Along with the call came a sharp tug on her hair that stopped Alicia as she filed out of her lecture class. She turned cautiously as the others stepped around and past her. It was her erstwhile swain from last weekend's party.

She was not completely surprised. She had noticed him in class trying to chat up an unresponsive blonde, oblivious to the irritated shushings around him. While mechanically taking notes on the Nihilism movement in Art, Alicia had found time to speculate on how well he might know Devereaux

Rafferty. He had called him 'Dev', but in that crowd, lack of formalities meant nothing. She couldn't connect Dev Rafferty with someone so transparently callow—but one could never tell.

'*Carrington!*' he mocked, twisting the long hair around his finger. Apparently he had lost his blonde prospective girl-friend. There he stood: tall, shaggy, and somehow self-assured. 'You ran out on me!' Students edged around them with glances of varying degrees of curiosity. It was nothing new.

'Ouch,' Alicia said automatically, knowing it was expected.

'I don't like being ditched,' he informed her loudly, but he was grinning. He gave her hair another tweak.

Alicia sighed and mustered up a feeble smile.

'Big deal meeting Rafferty, huh? You owe me, Carrington, and you owe me big!' She supposed underneath it all he was just a bad tease.

'Uh—I think we're blocking the door,' she said patiently, glancing around and trying not to pull her hair.

'So?' He tugged her hair sharply. 'Pay attention, kid!'

He still had that stupid self-satisfied smile on his face. Alicia was beginning to get annoyed. She widened her blue eyes as though impressed by this display of male dominance. 'I'm listening,' she protested.

'Yeah, well you'll want to hear this, I guess. This'll make your girlish heart flutter.' He leered down at her. 'Why I'm so nice to you when you ran out on me, I don't know.' He shook his shaggy yellow head. 'You want to get down to Maxwell's, babe. He's holding an exhibition.'

'He—who?' Alicia asked swiftly, suddenly alert.

'He who?' Alicia asked swiftly, suddenly alert.

'Dense!' mocked her friend, laughing maliciously, and shaking his head. 'Devereaux Lloyd what's-his-name. He's at Maxwell's, holding court. Americans, rich bitches and *Carringtons* only!'

'*Now?*' Already she was mentally rearranging her schedule.

'That's right—so what's it worth? Today's notes?'

She tore them out of her notebook, handing them over without a word. He released her hair to take them, laughing nastily.

'No problem for you, right? You just flash the old driver's ID and the hallowed portals fly open. Am I right?'

'Thanks!' Alicia ignored his sarcasm and scurried off across the lawn, clutching her books and deaf to his loud laughter behind her.

Her own excitement amazed her. She was a little old to be having crushes on hero-figures. All the same, she dumped her books into her car and drove straight to Maxwell's without stopping to change from jeans and bulky sweater. She never spared a thought for her Drawing class or lunch.

But when she reached the Gallery, feeling tense and a little foolish, there was an unexpected stumbling block. The receptionist in the spacious front hall was new and eyed Alicia's jean-clad, scruffy figure doubtfully.

'I'm sorry, but this is a private viewing,' she apologised with a practised smile.

'Is Mr Maxwell in?' Alicia demanded breathlessly.

The receptionist's thinly plucked brows rose.

Alicia jammed her hands into her sweater pockets, and colour mounting, said firmly, 'Please tell him

Alicia Carrington is at the front desk.' No doubt Jacqueline would have spoken more authoritatively, but the receptionist felt the assurance behind Alicia's soft voice. She reached for the buzzer and Alicia felt a small spark of achievement.

Behind them a white door flew open and Mr Maxwell himself strode into the lobby, laughing cheerfully at something his companion said. Catching sight of Alicia, he exclaimed delightedly, 'My dear Miss Carrington!'

His dear Miss Carrington barely noticed beaming Mr Maxwell. She focused over his short, portly figure on the lean graceful man with him, feeling no surprise, only a sense of realising destiny.

'Hullo,' Alicia said, smiling at Dev Rafferty. He nodded politely. He wore chocolate cords and a cream-coloured cashmere pullover that brought out the spring green of his eyes and the red glints in his wavy hair. The sheer vitality of his presence was almost overwhelming. He was just as she remembered, and it was hard to tear her eyes away. Years of training stood by her, however, and Alicia smiled shyly at Mr Maxwell, saying, 'Your receptionist tells me that you're having a private viewing.'

'Indeed we are. Indeed, yes. We'd be delighted if *you* would join us.' He nodded, smiling at his companion, and then exclaimed, '*What* am I thinking of? Devereaux Rafferty, Miss Alicia Carrington.'

'We've met,' Alicia responded.

Rafferty's brows drew together in quick perplexity. 'I'm sorry—?'

'At the party, Friday night.' Alicia was used to blending into the décor, but this was the first time she had ever felt happy about it; better to be forgotten than remembered only because of the Carrington millions.

'Of course.' His smile was rueful, but very charming. 'I've a terrible memory.' Alicia doubted it. She recognised another bit of casual kindness. 'You're a—student?' His expression was patient. She supposed he was used to putting up with youthful admirers, especially female.

She nodded, while Mr Maxwell bubbled enthusiastically, 'And one of our most generous patrons!' and tried not to wince.

Mr Maxwell offered another cheerful comment or two to which Alicia replied unimpressively, and then he ushered his prize artist off to a late lunch. Alicia went on into the show room. Several people strolled quietly up and down the long airy gallery pausing before various paintings to discuss their merits in hushed tones. January sunshine poured through the skylight: cold, bright and stark. Alicia hugged herself against a chill that was not merely physical and wandered over to the nearest wall. Examining the first painting, she was aware of curious glances from one or two fellow observers, and wished suddenly she had bothered to change. She looked like a kid.

But within a few seconds'-worth of scrutiny Alicia had forgotten her self-consciousness. Naturally she had seen Rafferty's work before, although it was different viewing it with a personal interest in the artist. She was impressed, but tried to study everything with critical detachment. He had a distinct style and flawless technique, but he varied between the modern and traditional with no strong base in either school. A New Wave Impressionist? Even Aunt Elizabeth would have recognised any of his subjects—revolutionary for a respectable Modern artist.

Choice of colour, texture, even subject evoked an uncanny response in Alicia. She *knew* what he had felt when he had painted, for example, that purple and yellow seascape; she thought she recognised the emotions, but how could someone like Dev Rafferty paint the world as someone like Alicia Carrington saw it? That, she knew, was what her instructors meant by the 'universal voice' of the truly great.

His work made her—for lack of a better word— hungry. Hungry to see and smell and touch what he had. Hungry to feel and live. Yes, that was perhaps the strongest impression she absorbed from his work: shining vibrant life. Something in Alicia's retiring, introspective nature rose up at the subtle nuance of shade and light, at the almost achingly bold colours. Her heart beat fast in response to her brain's stimulation—they were so beautiful! So overwhelming! What genius. What a wonderful man to feel like this and be able to bring it to life on canvas.

If only she knew someone like him. If only she could know *him*. But that was ridiculous. Devereaux Rafferty had no time or room in his life for mousy little schoolgirls. The woman he knew were like the woman in the portrait she stared at now, his companion the night of the party.

The door to the reception lobby opened and Alicia looked around hopefully, but it was not Rafferty and she turned back to the painting a little disappointed. However, the next moment she was too engrossed in the portrait to notice who went in or out. It was fascinating, in an uncomfortable sort of way. Robed in green, the woman was seated in shadow, her lovely face thrown up as though to be kissed. She looked sinuous, inviting, but her eyes were slits, the pupils alert and watching under the heavy white lids. She looked like a snake, a half-charmed cobra. Alicia recognised with half-amused shock that the resemblance was heightened by the lower half of her body painted in fluid, languid, almost slithery lines. The green robe trailed off into shadows like loose coils. Several minutes passed unnoticed while she studied.

'And what do you think,' a precise voice was drawling behind her, 'about the energy and attention in the New Art?'

'I don't know,' a familiar voice answered with lazy indifference. 'I never really thought about it.'

Alicia glanced around in time to see the interviewer give Rafferty a disbelieving look. Rafferty's bored gaze caught Alicia's and his mouth quivered slightly. Hastily Alicia turned back to the painting.

A moment later he stood beside her and Alicia held herself very still and straight, trying to cover her pleasure.

'Do you like that?' he asked, giving the portrait a jerk of chin.

'It's very good,' she said truthfully, keeping her eyes to the painting.

He laughed briefly. 'A well-bred child! I don't like it, either. I did at the time.' He sounded almost uneasy.

'How did *she* like it?' Alicia murmured, still concentrating on the portrait.

'She was amused.' He sounded amused also, pushing his hands into his pockets. 'Yes, sir, that's my baby,' he mused. Catching Alicia's sideways glance, his smile was quick and attractive. 'You know you ought to cut your hair.'

Alicia blinked. 'I ought?'

'It's an awkward length. Breaks the line of your body.' The bright green eyes were critical, but impersonal. 'Obscures your face, your bones, which is a pity.' Reaching out, he caught a thick shank of her hair in a loose fist, not pulling. 'Right about there,' he said, swinging it before Alicia's eyes. 'You see?' Alicia nodded and he loosed her, still smiling but perfectly serious. 'I expect you've been growing it for ever?'

Alicia laughed. Somehow he managed to be both impersonal and friendly so that what he said was neither insulting nor forward. Nor did he talk down. He was merely giving good advice.

'All right,' she said agreeably, to which he laughed again, although his eyes flickered in a way she didn't understand. There was a note in his laugh—it was kind, but it could easily have turned to sarcasm. She had the sudden feeling that he could, with very little effort, be very unkind, even cruel. Once more she looked nervously away.

However, before anything further could be said, Mr Maxwell joined them and—somewhat to Alicia's chagrin—apologetically drew Rafferty away to answer questions from *The Times*' Art Critic. Alicia decided she had lingered long enough and, after arranging to buy the seascape she had admired from the genial Mr Maxwell, went out with a brief, unnoticed glance at Dev Rafferty who was absorbed in conversation.

The next morning, before her courage had time to fail, Alicia made an appointment at the hair salon Jacqueline and Aunt Elizabeth frequented.

It was not nearly as traumatic an experience as she had expected. Mr André had itched for years to get his clever fingers on the younger Miss Carrington's mane. Now at last he had her where he wanted her, and wasted no time. With a few alarmingly loud snips of scissors Alicia had a shoulder-length blunt cut, and her chopped tresses lay on the floor looking drab and strange. Her calm satisfaction encouraged Mr André to suggest a fringe. He was so enthusiastic, and Alicia was still in the grip of adventurousness, so she agreed, and Mr André snipped cheerfully away, praising the condition and silky-fine texture of her hair.

Alicia was delighted with the result. The fringe softened her square face and emphasised her eyes. The shorter length played up her fine bones and the hollows in her cheeks. It was like magic. She eagerly accepted Mr André's next suggestion of blonde highlights, and found that the little gold ribbons enhanced her own hair colour. It was amazing. Alicia earnestly thanked him, which Mr André waved aside gallantly, and left the salon feeling like a new girl. A daring, adventurous sort of girl.

In her entire life she had never changed a single aspect of her appearance to impress any man. She was not trying to impress Dev Rafferty—she would probably never see him again—but she was thinking suddenly in terms of impressing someone *like* Rafferty. There was something about him that made Alicia, even in the scant two times she had met him, impatient with herself and her life. Even more impatient than she already was. It seemed to Alicia that she knew all about Dev Rafferty just by looking at his work—and she admired him immensely. Admired the arrogant confidence, the bold daring, the freedom. She would like to be like that some day, and her haircut seemed like a first step in the right direction.

Somehow it was a little dampening then that Aunt

Elizabeth should so thoroughly approve of the change.

'Very nice, dear,' she commented as Alicia obediently rotated before her. 'André did an excellent job.' It was worth something to have pleased Aunt Elizabeth. Alicia rarely managed it.

Laying aside the ledger of household accounts she had been studying (Aunt Elizabeth knew if even an extra loaf of bread went missing from her cupboards—the dishonest were not long employed at Carrington House) her aunt said briskly, 'I'm delighted to see you taking an interest in your personal appearance, Alicia. It shows a healthy sense of pride in self.'

Alicia folded her hands neatly in her lap, recognising from her aunt's tone that this was not a random comment, but a prelude. Her gaze wandered vaguely around her aunt's sitting room. It was not a precisely cosy room, there were no comfortable nooks and crannies in Aunt Elizabeth's character, but it was cool and comfortable, in an immaculate way. The furnishings were spare, but of the best quality, nearly all of them Victorian antiques collected by Alicia's great-grandparents. The room was too dark for Alicia's taste, and of course one had to be careful not to knock or spill in that room. The only incongruity was the television set perched on a spindly gilt table before the velvet sofa.

'You are a woman, now, Alicia. In a few years you will gain your full inheritance. I see no reason not to tell you that for some time this thought has worried me. You are rather immature for your age, and great wealth when not prudently handled can lead to disaster. Your money will make you a target for the unsavoury.' Aunt Elizabeth's pale blue eyes bored into Alicia's. 'In the past there has been nothing in your selection of friends, or your lack of ambition, to give me confidence that this was not your case.'

There had to be some point to this, Alicia reflected silently. Her aunt was obviously leading up to something. Uneasily, she smoothed her hands over the curved wooden handles of the chair, waiting.

'I hope that you are beginning to outgrow some of your more exhausting and youthful ideas?'

'I hope so,' Alicia said doubtfully.

'I think you will find life a great deal easier when you have given up notions of rebellion.'

'I don't mean to be rebellious,' Alicia began, but was cut short by her aunt's brisk:

'In any case that was not what I wished to discuss. Your sister Jacqueline has suggested a Carribbean cruise in April. I think it would do us all good to get away for a week or two.'

'I couldn't afford to take that much time off from school,' Alicia objected. She heard the protest in her voice and winced. Helpless frustration would not avail against her aunt. She must strive for assurance. 'But the two of you could go,' she added quickly.

The silence was pregnant. Aunt Elizabeth's features tightened as though Alicia had made a joke in bad taste.

'I see.' There was something ominous in her tone.

'I can't take off so near graduation,' Alicia explained.

'You won't, rather.'

'All right then, I won't!' Alicia exclaimed agitatedly. 'I've worked too long and too hard.'

'A selfish attitude, as I'm sure you're aware of.'

Alicia swallowed. 'I—I'm sorry you feel that, but my staying needn't affect the trip. I'm twenty-three years old—'

Aunt Elizabeth's hand moved dismissingly and Alicia stopped short.

'Your attitude indicates clearly to me that you are not responsible enough to be left unsupervised for several weeks.'

Alicia rose, biting back shaky anger with difficulty. 'I'm sorry you think so.'

Aunt Elizabeth's head bent as she pulled the ledger back across the writing desk. Alicia stumbled out without another word.

Upstairs in her bedroom, staring at the grey sky outside the window, Alicia wondered despairingly how she could possibly get through the next two years. It was all very well to think in terms of new beginnings and being positive and forceful, but it just didn't *work*. Forlornly she tried to imagine how Devereaux Rafferty would deal with someone like Aunt Elizabeth, but she couldn't imagine him knowing anyone like her aunt. She couldn't picture him with family ties at all. He seemed utterly, ideally independent.

How did people become like that? Was it in-born? Was it environment? Jacqueline had grown up in the same environment, but there was nothing timid or spineless about Jacqueline. Alicia dropped her head in her hands, pressing her fingers against her burning eyes. She thought of going downstairs to dinner and felt ill. There was nowhere she could go. No one she could turn to for advice. If she knew someone like Dev Rafferty it would be different. What a lot one could learn by example. Just seeing him made her feel more brave.

But there were no Dev Raffertys in Alicia Carrington's life. Nor, if Aunt Elizabeth had her way, would there be. It wouldn't end here, Alicia knew. This was but a preliminary skirmish—Aunt Elizabeth was preparing to mount a full-scale offensive over this Caribbean cruise. She wouldn't stop until she had booked Alicia's passage. Alicia groaned and, rising, crossed over the room, throwing herself flat on the neatly made pink silk bedspread. She didn't cry. She was not a 'crier'. She buried her face in the cool softness and tried to think of other ways to meet Dev Rafferty to cheer herself up.

In the old days it would have been simple. She could have been a patron. She could have commissioned him . . . Slowly Alicia raised her head. Commission? Why not? It wasn't such a far-fetched idea. He must do some work by commission. She held her breath, considering excitedly the possibility. At the least, she would get to talk to him again. She sat up, brushing back her hair absently, surprised at its shortness. She had nothing to lose by trying after all . . . Feeling much more hopeful, Alicia rose and began changing for dinner.

It took her over a week to build up the nerve to act on her impulsive idea of commissioning Devereaux Rafferty to paint her portrait. In the end it was the arrival of the seascape she had bought at the Maxwell exhibition that spurred Alicia into action. She had forgotten how throbbingly beautiful the painting was, with its silky pale sand, jagged blue-brown rocks and a tumbled grey sea reflecting the molten dawn. Alicia had Joseph, the gardener, hang it for her across from her bed so that she could wake to it every morning. It only took one morning before she was filled again with the restless, hungry impatience for life, the impact of the painting.

Putting aside her characteristic backwardness,

Alicia went to see Mr Maxwell at the Gallery to gain his help in contacting Rafferty.

It was obvious that Mr Maxwell had his doubts about Alicia's plan. He listened with his habitual bird-bright intensity, nodding, but when she finished, he said slowly:

'Yes, of course, a wonderful investment, and a lovely, thoughtful gift for your aunt, but Rafferty rarely does portraits, my dear Miss Carrington— and very rarely does he do commissions these days.'

'You think it's no use?' Alicia asked, patently disappointed.

Mr Maxwell hesitated. 'It's hard to say. He's a temperamental creature in many ways, the truly brilliant tend to be.' He smiled his winning smile. 'We have nothing to lose by asking.'

At Alicia's request he gave the number and she thanked him and went away—the paper with Dev Rafferty's name and address on it, figuratively burning a hole in her pocket.

Alicia didn't have any particular plan. She thought she had a better chance of being accepted if she went to see Rafferty in person. Besides, she wanted to see him, not just hear his distant voice over a phone line. So she drove down to the address given the same day, before she had time to change her mind again.

Rafferty rented rooms at the top of a Victorian renovated mansion. The building was enormous and somewhat dilapidated, one of the last of its era, crammed between shops and skyrises; a little piece of old London struggling to hold ground against the new. It was not a good neighbourhood: crowded, noisy and plagued by constant traffic. It did not fit Alicia's mental image of Dev Rafferty.

Firmly she mounted the long, winding staircase to the top and knocked briskly on his door. She was too absorbed by the peculiar smells and sights around her to be nervous. Dark and drafty inside, outside the traffic rumbled. From below wafted the smell of curry.

There was no answer. Alicia knocked again loudly, and the door opened.

'Yes?' It was that simple. There he stood in a calf-length dark green dressing gown, looking at Alicia a little impatiently, with narrowed eyes.

'Mr Rafferty,' she stumbled, 'I'm Alicia Carrington. I bought your seascape at Maxwell's a few weeks ago—' She had forgotten how overwhelmingly vivid his presence was. Dimly she wondered how she had had the nerve to come.

'I remember,' he interrupted. 'The girl with the Victorian name.' He smiled fleetingly, but his eyes stayed hard. Alicia received the impression that he was angry, very angry and trying hard to control it. She blinked nervously at him, and he added speculatively, 'I like the fringe.'

From inside the flat a door slammed and out of the corner of her eye Alicia saw something sail past behind Rafferty's head, smashing against the far wall. He jerked around at the crash and Alicia's ears caught a woman's muffled raving. She couldn't quite pick out the words, but Rafferty said in a clear, even voice, 'Don't let me stop you. Why not use the window?'

There was another wall-shaking door slam and Rafferty turned back to Alicia. He took in her enormous eyes and said sardonically, 'She tends to be a bit moody before her morning coffee.' It wasn't funny to him, though, Alicia sensed.

'I'll come back later,' she offered, starting to back away.

'Oh no.' He followed her out on to the landing, drawing the dressing gown around him absently. The idea that he wasn't wearing anything underneath occurred to Alicia. She lowered her gaze to his feet as he shut the door behind him. Even they were slender and well-shaped.

'We can talk in my studio,' he was saying, and she padded after him down the dank, dark hall, her spirits lifting.

He unlocked a door and she followed him into a long, airy room. Sunlight poured in through the glassed roof, and the smell of turpentine assaulted Alicia's nose. There were white canvases stacked in one corner, and painted canvases drying on easels or against walls. Rags and paint and pads with preliminary sketches were scattered everywhere; but it was not messy, merely disorganised. Alicia liked it immediately. It had a comfortable, productive feel.

Crossing to a door at the far end, which Alicia guessed adjoined his living quarters, Rafferty locked it, and threw her a rueful glance. She was glad he didn't apologise and make her feel stuffy and conservative.

'Have you been married long?' she asked politely, for the sake of something to say.

'We're not married.' At her instantly expressionless face, he said mockingly, 'The name suits you.'

She remembered he had called her name Victorian and she explained, 'I'm surprised that she would behave like that when there's nothing to stop ·
you from leaving.'

His amusement increased. 'I think I'll have you talk to her.' He tipped some papers off a chair and pushed it towards her. 'Well, Alicia Carrington, what can I do for you?' His tone was brisk.

Alicia obediently seated herself, looking up at him. He studied her with candid interest, not impatiently but curiously. She guessed that he would be kind but thorough in dealing with unwanted attention from adoring fans. She said in businesslike accents, 'I'd like to commission you to paint my portrait—for my Aunt Elizabeth's birthday in March. I spoke to Mr Maxwell about it. He said you almost never painted portraits, but I thought you might.' She paused and tried not to look too hopeful.

'Did you? Why?' he inquired.

Alicia smiled. This was her ace card. 'You said you would,' she answered simply.

'I did? When?' He was smiling back, still amused.

'At that party where we first met. You said I had good bones and character.'

'Did I? Well, so you have. It's an interesting face—although you don't play it up enough.' He regarded Alicia meditatively and she gazed steadily back. Long seconds ticked by while he considered. 'Why not?' he said abruptly and shrugged.

Alicia's mouth dropped. 'You mean you will?' she uttered disbelievingly. It was the last thing she had expected and she was frankly stunned.

His brows shot up at her evident shock. 'If the price is right, why not?' he said cynically. She flushed slightly at that, which he took in with those cool, hard eyes. After a moment, he added more kindly, 'Anyway, it's a good face. I'd like to paint it.'

Alicia cast him a brief, shy look. Mr Maxwell had implied that artistic integrity kept Rafferty from commissioning out. He didn't sound quite so ethical, but she supposed he had to make a living. Instinctively she felt that he would shy away at any suggestion of nobility or virtuousness.

'The price doesn't matter.' She hoped that didn't sound boastful or pushy. His eyes narrowed slightly.

'That's very tempting, however I think we can work something fair out.' He rubbed his cheek, eyeing her, and Alicia rushed in;

'When would you like me to come and sit?'

He continued to rub his cheek contemplatively before suggesting, 'Monday? Ten o'clock?'

'All right. I've got class at three. Will we be done by then?'

This seemed to amuse him. 'We'll finish in plenty of time,' he assured her gravely.

'Thank you.' She felt again that he was almost making fun of her, and her eyes met his unwaveringly as she rose, offering her hand.

He smiled, taking it. She felt the strength in his clasp, although his hand was fine and slender.

'Thank *you*,' he returned urbanely. He saw her to the door and Alicia went past him into the dim hallway feeling incredibly lucky. Monday seemed years away, but at least there was going to be Monday. She was very conscious of his eyes following her down the hall.

'And for God's sake wear something bright,' he called after her as she started down the stairs.

'I will!' Alicia called back happily, clattering down the steps.

CHAPTER TWO

ALICIA was five minutes late, arriving breathlessly at the studio to find the door open and Dev Rafferty inside drinking from a mug and staring out the window at the busy street below.

'I'm awfully sorry!' she gasped out. He turned around, his brows raising inquiringly. His grim expression faded slightly. Alicia hastened to apologise, 'It was the vet. He came late.'

'What was the vet?' he queried.

'The cause of my being late,' explained Alicia.

'Late?' He glanced at his watch. 'So you are.' Clearly whatever gave him that hard-faced look had nothing to do with her. Alicia dropped her satchel against the wall and shifted weight awkwardly. He smiled at her suddenly.

'What's the matter?'

'Matter?' she blinked nervously.

'You look lost.'

'Oh. No.' She shrugged and smiled back. 'I thought you might be annoyed about my being late.'

'What, five minutes?' He laughed disbelievingly. Then, taking in her apparel, his face grew resigned. Alicia glanced down self-deprecatingly. She hadn't had much to choose from, and she knew the navy blue skirt and pale pink blouse were not what Rafferty had in mind by 'bright'.

'I don't bother much about clothing,' she apologised.

'That is obvious.' He frowned slightly. 'Who picks your things? How old are you anyway?'

'Twenty-three.' She said it defensively.

His tilted eyes widened. 'Twenty-three? Good God. I imagined you were about nineteen.' There was a silence.

'I guess I am backward for my age,' Alicia admitted. 'Most girls my age——'

'Most girls your age wouldn't be up here,' he interrupted flatly. 'You're here because you're different. I don't paint just anybody.' It was said with a somehow cheering arrogance. 'All the same——' he weighed her up beneath lowered lids, '——we're not going to present you to posterity in those clothes.'

'I could go home and change.'

'What would you change into?'

'I have a cream——'

He shook his head. 'No. I know what I see you in. Come with me.'

Doubtful but curious, she followed him down the long, dark narrow stairs out into the sunlit, crowded pavement. Tagging behind, she followed down the street and into the shabby-looking antique-pawn shop he dived into without pause. She made her way up the crowded, jumbled aisle to find Dev Rafferty already conversing with the proprietor.

'There you are,' he said, as though she had been hours behind. They waited silently as the shop owner brought them a bundle of violet silk from the back room. Dev Rafferty took it from him, shaking it out with a magicianlike snap. It was a dress, a dress of incredible colour, rich but muted. The silk was threadbare in parts but, in all, the garment was in excellent shape. The style was very Victorian: the high throat and long sleeves edged with fine lace, the bodice fastened with tiny pearl buttons.

'It might be a little short, but we only need the top half. Luckily you're thin,' Dev Rafferty commented over his shoulder.

Alicia nodded, opening her wallet.

'Never mind that,' he said brusquely, and Alicia blinked at him in surprise.

'But—'

'Don't be silly.'

'But it's for my portrait.' She gave the proprietor a sheepish look. Dev Rafferty shot her an impatient glance while the man waited.

'Call it a sort of present. Now shut up.'

So Alicia stood silently while he paid for the antique dress, buying a violet ribbon as well. No one had ever bought her anything before, except on Christmas and birthdays. Never anything spontaneously, and never from anyone who hadn't as much money as Alicia. She felt that it was an exceptional gesture for someone to insist on buying her something so unnecessary—knowing she had so much more money. Most people took it for granted Alicia would pay.

As Dev Rafferty handed her the package something sparked to life within Alicia. The feeling was unknown, but it was something Aunt Elizabeth would have recognised and gained no comfort from knowing.

The dress was a near fit: short, but comfortably loose through the waist, hips and bust. The arms weren't quite long enough, but Rafferty liked the effect of her thin, brown wrists peeping out from the lace cuffs. He seated Alicia by the window, positioning her so that she leant against the sill, arms resting on the white surface.

'Now look over your shoulder,' he commanded.

Alicia looked. It wasn't an easy pose to hold.

'Straighten up,' Rafferty snapped. Alicia arched her back obligingly. 'Good. Okay, relax. We'll do your hair.'

'My hair?' Alicia sat back gratefully as he hunted up a comb from the desk drawer's jumbled contents. Standing over Alicia, he ran it lightly through her hair. His fingers were cool and gentle at her nape. She shut her eyes and let her head tilt forward. His impersonal caress sent little thrills of delighted sensation over her.

'Don't fall asleep,' he warned, amused. He brushed her hair in a loose sweep to the side of her head and fastened it with the velvet ribbon he had bought, so that the plait hung over her fair shoulder. 'That'll do.'

He moved away, and Alicia was aware of regret.

'Assume the position,' he ordered, picking up his sketch pad. Alicia straightened, turned her head and tilted her chin as he had shown her. She was rewarded by a charming smile.

The first hour passed and Alicia had a five-minute break. For the next two hours Rafferty worked in silence. Once he muttered something and tore off a sheet crumpling it into a ball. Alicia knew it was stupid to take it personally, but it added to her tension. Her muscles ached. It was hard to sit unmoving for so long.

'Hold still, please,' Dev Rafferty said mechanically. Alicia gritted her teeth and hung on. Another fifteen minutes passed before he sighed and said abruptly, 'You can move if you like.'

If she liked? If she could. Alicia stretched cautiously and stood up.

'What time is it?' Rafferty asked absently, fingers still busy.

Alicia picked her wrist watch up from the sill—Rafferty didn't want it in the painting. 'Two-fifteen. I've got to go!' She pulled the ribbon out of her hair and wriggled around trying to unbutton the dress. He laid aside the pad.

'Hold still.' He undid the buttons with practised speed, his fingers warm against her bare skin. Again Alicia was aware of delightful sensations. Rafferty remarked prosaically, 'I ought to pay you overtime.'

'I'm paying you,' Alicia pointed out.

He grinned. 'Maybe you should pay me overtime.'

Alicia chuckled, hurrying through the door to the flat in order to change. When she returned to retrieve her books he was sitting with his feet on the desk, chair tilted back, stretching. He nodded an absent farewell to her bright;

'Well, see you Thursday!'

Alicia went down the staircase strangely feeling a little disappointed.

He was a difficult person to know; sometimes moody and sharp with nerves; sometimes closed and cynical; sometimes kind and amused. He could be mocking, but he was never sarcastic; he could be irritable without coldness; and he could be arrogant without belittling Alicia. None of the character defects in her that drove Jacqueline and Aunt Elizabeth sharp with exasperation seemed to bother him. He didn't snap about punctuality or clumsiness or less than brilliant conversation. All he cared about was the painting. Art. Alicia knew Dev Rafferty had faults, but they seemed minimal compared to his gifts. Alicia eagerly anticipated every session and lamented how quickly the few hours a week flew by. She still hoped to learn the secret of his confident individuality by listening and watching carefully, but none of it seemed to rub off.

She would have liked to stay after her sessions, but she was afraid of pestering him, so as soon as the afternoon's painting was done she changed hurriedly and left.

She did not see much of Magda Morrison, the vile-tempered beauty he lived with. Her belongings scattered the flat when Alicia went to change, and she learned that Magda, a sculptress, had a studio of her own in town.

Once Alicia came in a minute or two early to find the studio empty, the adjoining door open, and loud voices coming from the flat.

'I am sick to death of your *Art*,' Magda's voice came clearly. 'I'm an artist, too! Do you think your needs always come first? What about *my* needs? You couldn't care less! You've never given a damn about anybody else in your life.'

'Louder, Magda,' Dev Rafferty's voice snarled back. 'The people across the street can't quite hear.'

'God! And now middle-class attitudes! What will the neighbours think! What's next, teaching art at the Royal Academy?'

'Oh, go to hell.' He sounded fed up, his voice nearer to the door and Alicia, transfixed with embarrassment, looked around for some way to make her presence known. She set down her satchel with a thud on the floor and cleared her throat, but this was drowned out by the hall door slamming.

The next moment Dev Rafferty strode into the

studio and slammed shut the connecting door. His eyes fell on red-faced Alicia.

'What the—? When did you get in?'

'Just a minute ago—I'm sorry,' she added pleadingly. 'I didn't mean to overhear.'

His laugh was short and nasty. 'How could you help it?' He flung himself over to the desk, opened a drawer and banged it shut. The sheer violence in his movements made Alicia wince.

'Should I come back later?'

'Why? She'll be gone for the afternoon and half the night.'

Alicia wondered if that sounded like she thought it did. Unaccountably she felt depressed when he added, 'And by tomorrow it will all have blown over.'

'Oh.'

He ignored her, drumming his fingers restlessly on the desk top, then glanced up and bit out impatiently, 'What are you standing around for? Get changed!'

'Sorry.' Alicia collected herself and went hastily next door to undress. When she returned to the studio he was in front of the easel, mixing the palette. She crossed over to the window and resumed her pose without a word.

It was a long session and nothing seemed to please Dev Rafferty who snapped and swore at her the entire time. 'Straighten up! For God's sake what's wrong with your face? It's all stiff. Loosen up! Raise your chin. Can we have some kind of expression, please? Any at all will do.' On and on. Alicia gritted her teeth and struggled to do as he asked, but nothing helped. Finally, he broke off the session in exasperation, and feeling to blame Alicia went back next door to change clothes.

When she returned to the studio he was looking out of the rain-glistening, foggy window. He glanced over his shoulder and said briskly, 'You may as well stay and have a hot drink. At least till the rain lets up.'

It was the unexpected, long-hoped-for invitation Alicia had waited for, but in this mood of Dev Rafferty's, she wasn't so sure.

'If I won't disturb you—?' she began cautiously.

'I'm already disturbed, you may have noticed.' But he grinned faintly.

She followed him back into the flat's kitchen which was a mess of dirty dishes with a paper-strewn table. She was vaguely shocked. There was something sordid about left-over breakfast in the dim afternoon light.

'Yes, it must be a change,' he commented, his green eyes flickeringly taking in her surprise. 'It's always educational to see how the other half live.' His inflection was self-mocking, but Alicia reddened. He made her feel prudish and spoilt.

'It must be nice to have your own place.'

'At thirty-four the novelty has worn off.' He sounded amused again, clearing a space on the table and wiping it efficiently. He fished through the cupboard for clean mugs and put a pan of milk on the stove. This was one of the bits of personal information Alicia had gleaned: that he preferred chocolate to coffee or tea. She knew also that he hated TV, read voraciously, was allergic to cats and detested smoking, although Magda indulged. Each little piece of information discovered was pasted away by Alicia in her scrap-book memory.

'Why are you still living at home, Alicia, if you

don't want to?' Rafferty inquired, his back to her as
Alicia settled herself at the table.

'I won't come into my money until I'm twenty-
five, or marry. Until then my Aunt Elizabeth con-
trols my allowance and she won't hear of my moving
out.'

'Ah. Money. The necessary evil.' His voice was
lightly grim.

'I can't get a job while I'm in school and the school
means a better job. So I just have to wait.' She
sighed.

'Your aunt raised you?'

'Yes, my parents died when I was a baby. Aunt
Elizabeth raised me and my sister singlehandedly.
My sister married a few years ago and now there's
just me.'

He didn't comment on her careful tone, saying
instead, 'We've something in common. My parents
died when I was in my teens.'

'I'm sorry.' That must have been hard, to lose
them at that sensitive age. She said slowly, 'Were
they artistic?'

He gave a brief laugh. 'Certainly. He was Irish,
she was French and together they enjoyed a number
of romantic illusions. They lived like something out
of a Thirties film about the happy penniless artist;
complete in each other and their "artistic vision".'
There was a cynicism in that that startled Alicia, as
though he scorned them for being happy in their
poverty. 'So you see,' he added, 'it's in the blood.'

'Artistic vision?'

'Failure.' He laughed at her expression. 'Isn't it
disillusioning to discover how one's been *worshipping*
clay feet?'

Until that moment Alicia had not realised how

obvious her admiration of him was, how plain for the world to see—so plain that he could make a little joke about it, as though it were perfectly natural that she should worship him. A wave of hot humiliation rushed over Alicia. She rose shakily. 'I think the rain's stopped—' she got out.

'Don't be silly. You haven't had your cocoa.' He spoke chidingly, as to a child, not even watching her, and Alicia was suddenly resentful.

'I have to go,' she said shortly.

He turned to her, his attention caught by her inflection. 'What's up?'

'Nothing. I have a date.'

'Ah.' He nodded. To Alicia's surprise he accepted that. 'Well, he can wait five minutes while you have a hot drink.' He brought her mug over, and overwhelmed at the possible ramifications of her lie, Alicia sat back down and drank the cocoa, eyes fastened on the rim.

Dev Rafferty drank slowly, staring out of the window over the kitchen sink. Reluctantly Alicia found herself wondering about the mornings he spent sitting here with Magda. She didn't like what little she saw of Magda, but she could see why someone like Dev Rafferty needed a woman as exciting and exotic as himself.

'This weather reminds me of Scotland,' he remarked lazily after a moment or two.

Alicia had been once or twice to Scotland for the grouse hunt. She imagined Dev Rafferty had had a vastly different experience of the place.

'Have you been there often?' she asked, her former ire dimming.

'Only once, for a summer when I was about your age. A friend and I went up to the Highlands to paint. We stayed in an old croft and lived on oatcakes and trout.' He grinned slightly at the memory. 'They said it was the wettest summer they'd had in years.'

From things he had said she knew that he had been all over the world: Southern France, Egypt, Ireland, Spain, Greece. Fascinating, extraordinary places that Alicia had only read about. One day, when she had her inheritance, she was going to travel, too. Till then she would have to wait. It was no use going with Aunt Elizabeth and Jacqueline; their idea of foreign travel was to lounge by the pool of a cruise-ship for six weeks.

'It must have been nice,' she sighed wistfully and his brilliant eyes slid over to hers.

'Nice? I suppose so.' Nice seemed a mundane sort of word, Alicia reflected. Placid and boring, reeking of middle-class attitudes as Magda put it. Devereaux Rafferty was not a 'nice' person. She was feeling her own 'niceness' with a vengeance. Alicia set her mug down with a little bang and stood up again.

'I really must go,' she said.

He looked entertained again and she knew he thought she was nervously anticipating her 'date'. Again she resented his superior attitude. He rose, seeing her to the door of the flat, giving her a goodbye warning about driving in the rain as though she were a reckless teenager.

She drove home faster than usual, perhaps with some vague idea of 'showing' him, but when Alicia reached Carrington House her spirits took another drop. She stared at the white shuttered face of the house as she hurried up the stone walk steps. It looked prim, tight-lipped.

Lying in the darkness of her room, between the pristine sheets, Alicia listening to rain rattle the windows with needle-pricks of sound. For the first time, being around Dev Rafferty had depressed her. She wasn't sure why. Then she thought drearily, because he made her feel her loneliness. In one off-hand remark he revealed how he thought of her. Not as a friend, but as an idolising child. It was discouraging, disheartening. But what had she expected? That her life would change by having her portrait painted?

February, though grey and wet, was brightened for Alicia by her days at Dev Rafferty's studio. The painting progressed swiftly, almost too swiftly in Alicia's opinion. Sessions with Dev Rafferty began to form the crux of her regimented world.

Sometimes it seemed to Alicia she was leading a double life. On the surface she remained Alicia Carrington, pursuing the expected responsibilities of a young woman of name and fortune—without pleasure or particular ability. She only truly came to life when she was seated in Dev Rafferty's studio listening to him discuss Art or offer some anecdote from his past. Alicia couldn't remember any other place she felt as comfortable in or anyone she admired so much.

Nearly two weeks later, Dev Rafferty looked up from putting finishing touches on the canvas and said briskly, 'Come and look.'

Alicia stood up. Lifting the silk folds around her, she crossed to Dev and stood staring in astonishment at the canvas. 'It's beautiful—but it's not me!'

'It's exactly you,' he said, offended.

Uncertainly Alicia studied the portrait, wrinkling her nose. It *was* her—but it wasn't. The girl looking back from the window had a mischievous, almost inviting look. She was very pretty. Alicia bent closer trying to see what Dev Rafferty had actually done. The body was hers, lean, brown and taut in the ill-fitting silk. The hair was hers, although the style was not, managing to be both untidy and provocative. The face—it was certainly her face: her wide blue eyes, her small straight nose, her stubborn chin, her rosy pink mouth . . .

'You've made me up!' she accused. Eyes, cheeks, mouth were all flushed with delicate colour. Her lashes were darker, emphasising the blue of her eyes.

'Artistic licence,' Rafferty said slowly. 'If you prefer, I can mute the colouring.'

'Oh no,' Alicia murmured. 'I like her.' She turned to him, trying not to sound serious. 'Is that how you see me?'

'Mm.' For some reason he looked uneasy. He stared at the portrait as though seeking guidance.

'If I wore make-up,' Alicia said slowly, eyes on his beautiful profile, 'do you suppose I would be as attractive as that girl?'

'That girl *is* you,' he said impatiently, turning to Alicia. His strange green eyes stared into Alicia's grave blue ones. Then, as though hypnotised, almost unwillingly, his head bent. His lips touched hers in a cool, almost curious kiss. An odd sensation ran through Alicia. Her legs actually felt weak, her heart pounded fiercely. *It's true what those books say*, she thought feebly.

'I think this is my cue,' a clear voice said mockingly from behind them.

Dev Rafferty pulled back instantly, turning to where Magda lounged in the studio doorway. Alicia sat down weakly on the hard desk behind her. She

felt very breathless, but whether from embarrassment or the kiss, she wasn't sure.

'Back so soon?' Dev asked steadily, hands sliding
nonchalantly into his pockets.

'Not soon enough, apparently,' Magda returned.
She strolled into the studio, coming to where they
stood before the painting. She was smiling, but there
was a glitter in her violet eyes Alicia didn't like. She
felt the hair on the back of her neck prickle as Magda
paused beside her, tilting her head from side to side
as she appraised the painting.

'My, my,' she murmured, slanting Alicia a mocking look. 'Real life doesn't do you justice.'

Alicia understood why Dev had painted her as a
snake. She was small and beautiful—and quite deadly. She studied them both now, quite outsized but
perfectly self-assured. They stared back fascinated.

'All things considered, I'm not really surprised,'
commented Magda lazily. In her black velvet trous-
ers and scarlet silk shirt she managed to make Alicia,
in tattered costume, feel gawky and foolish.

'I'm sorry,' Alicia said before she knew it. Magda
had a right to be furious, but she needn't sound *so*
abject.

Magda allowed herself a slight smile. 'My *dear*, I
don't imagine for a moment *you* had anything to do
with this.' Her eyes moved caressingly over Dev's
expressionless face, saying gently, 'You run along
home.'

For a crazy instant Alicia thought she was talking
to Dev. Then she snapped out of her trance and
grabbed her things.

'Go ahead and change next door,' Dev told her in a
natural tone, forestalling her flight to the street
below in the threadbare gown.

Alicia obeyed, practically fleeing next door, wriggling out of the dress, not caring if she tore it, pulling on her own clothes with shaking fingers. Her feelings were too chaotic to allow her to think. She was only a little calmer when she returned to the studio. Magda was comfortably perched on a chair, while Dev was staring grimly out of the window. He turned at Alicia's entrance.

'Come back tomorrow, about three,' he said, sounding very much like always. He actually smiled at her, eyes mocking her embarrassment.

Relieved, Alicia smiled back eagerly, nodding agreement. Then she caught the listening stillness on Magda's face and her heart froze. She had the terrible feeling she was leaving something fragile and priceless in the reach of an enemy. Walking out of the studio was one of the hardest things she had ever done.

CHAPTER THREE

ALICIA spent a long, troubled night tossing and turning, trying to empty her mind of its disturbing pictures. Again and again she relived the moment Dev had kissed her, her lips tingling with memory. Again and again she relived Magda's appearance. Her face burned. It was so sordid, so clichéd: caught kissing the artist in his studio by his mistress.

The afternoon seemed to take days to materialise, but finally it was time to drive to the studio, which Alicia did with a combination of reluctance and excitement.

She slid out of her car, and dodging a half-soggy newspaper skidding down the street, went straight into the dark building. The smell of frying fish and tinny rock music assaulted her senses as she went briskly up the stairway.

When she reached the top level the studio door was shut, and Alicia was filled with disappointment. Timidly, she tapped at its scratched, peeling surface. There was no answer. She tried the handle and it turned under her fingers. The door swung open and Alicia walked into the room.

Everything looked much as she had left it, except that it was now empty of anyone but herself. Dingy cold light crept through the skylight and windows, sulking in the room's shadowy corners. In the depressing gloom everything looked shabby and forlorn. The room was cold as well. Alicia shivered, then went rigid as her eyes focused on the easel where her portrait stood. She stepped forward, unbelieving. The painting had been slashed in half, the portions rolling from the separation: Alicia brushed the torn canvas flat with a surprisingly steady hand. Maliciously her head was cut from her shoulders. Her painted face stared up, still smiling at its private little joke. Alicia felt sick.

'Damn!' Dev spoke from behind her. Alicia turned. He was standing in the adjoining doorway, looking tired and tense. 'I wanted to prepare you first.'

'How could she do such a thing?' Alicia questioned fiercely.

'If it makes you feel any better, that was aimed at me, not you.'

'Well, it doesn't!' She stared at the canvas in her hands, shaky with anger.

'I know it's disappointing for you—'

'That woman is dangerous!' Alicia interrupted.

The faintest of smiles came to his eyes. 'Occasionally. At any rate you don't have to worry. She's gone, bag and baggage.'

Alicia's anger died in the wake of a new, less easily defined emotion. 'She has?'

'I threw her out—' his eyes flickered. '—after I found this.'

'Out of the window, I hope,' Alicia groused.

He ignored that, saying, 'Unfortunately, it doesn't mend the damage.' He took the torn canvas from Alicia, his jaw tightening. She had never seen him really furious. Even now he was holding back a little.

Alicia said hesitantly, 'Could—could you repaint it?'

'Don't be ridiculous!' he bit out, in a kind of

outrage. 'What do you think I am, a bloody paint-by-number machine?'

She quailed. 'I wasn't thinking. Naturally you can't repaint it.' There didn't seem to be much else to say. She looked at his tense silent figure and said awkwardly, 'I'd better go.'

'What do you mean?' He looked at her with quick surprise.

'I mean, there's no point standing here staring at a ripped up picture!' Tension made her voice sharp. She shrugged.

'I can paint a new one,' he said impatiently.

Alicia looked up, relief flooding her face.

'What were you thinking?' he asked, puzzled, watching.

'I thought it was *me*. That you didn't want to spend so much time repainting me.'

He blinked. 'Why wouldn't I?'

'It would be boring for you, painting the same face—my face—all over again.'

'I like painting your face,' he said flatly. 'If I didn't I wouldn't have agreed the first time to paint you.'

'Oh. Well!' She stared at her shoes and cleared her throat.

'What's wrong now?' He sounded teasing, indulgent. She shot him a quick look. He wore a quizzical half-frowning expression as he studied her. 'Can I take a guess?'

Her eyes widened and he said amusedly, 'Is it to do with my kissing you?'

She wished he hadn't mentioned it. It lessened its importance, somehow.

'Will it calm your fears of I give you my word to keep my distance?' His tone was gently mocking. It exasperated Alicia. He just did not understand—but maybe that was best. There was more dignity in behaving with outraged modesty than slavish hero-worship. More suitable for a Carrington.

'It's not necessary,' she said.

'We don't want to make the boy-friend jealous,' he added, teasing.

'Boy-friend? *Oh.*' She considered quickly and sighed. 'That didn't work out.'

'I'm sorry.' He had that frustratingly kind note again.

Alicia said to shock him, 'No, he only cared about the money.'

'What?' Dev Rafferty's eyes narrowed.

'Yes,' Alicia said airily. 'I can always tell. I'm a good judge of character.'

His eyes were very green and made her suddenly uncomfortable. 'Can you? Well—good for you! Now, let's figure how we're going to do this . . .' He gave her a small push towards the flat's dressing quarters.

Aunt Elizabeth began the second stage of her Carib-bean cruise campaign about a week after Dev Raf-ferty began painting the second portrait of Alicia.

She brought it up one afternoon over lunch, in-quiring in a deceptively reasonable tone, 'Why is it so important to you to have this degree, Alicia? Why precisely now?'

'I'd like to get it done. I've delayed long enough. Besides, I'd have to take all these classes over.'

'I see. And what is your urgent need for this degree? Do you intend to get a job right away?'

'Well—yes.'

'I see. And why do you need this job—this career?'

'I'd like to be independent.'

'Of what?' This was the crux of the matter. Aunt

Elizabeth's eyes were cold and assessing as Alicia struggled to answer. 'You are already financially independent, or will be when you are twenty-five. Do you intend to renounce your fortune.'

'No . . .'

'No? Then equally I assume you do not intend to renounce your name and family?'

'Of course not.' She felt like an unfortunate defendant facing the court prosecutor.

'So it is not of these you wish to be independent?'

'No! I just want to accomplish something. I'd like to have a career. It would make me feel worthwhile.'

Aunt Elizabeth looked faintly scornful. 'It is not a career which makes a person worthwhile. One either is, or is not a worthwhile person. Do you consider yourself *not* to be a worthwhile person?'

'Yes—I mean, n-no. I don't know! I don't feel like there's any purpose to my life.'

Aunt Elizabeth put her vichyssoise spoon down sharply. 'Your "purpose" is to fulfil your duty to the name of Carrington. You would feel "worthwhile" if you had met your responsibilities as your sister did at your age. Children make you worthwhile. If you were married, your responsibilities would be as much career as you could possibly handle!'

'Who would I marry?' Alicia burst out.

'What is that supposed to mean? You're a Carrington—'

'And *what* does this have to do with a Caribbean cruise?' cried Alicia in bitter frustration.

Aunt Elizabeth stood up, her face flushed with anger. 'I will not tolerate impertinence from you, Alicia!' she said furiously, from her end of the long linen-covered table.

Alicia rose, too, her legs trembling. 'I don't mean to

be impertinent,' she choked out, 'but I am not going
on that cruise. I'm going to finish my schooling.'

'You may leave this room, Alicia,' Aunt Elizabeth
snapped out.

Alicia gave her a long, glittering look, then turned
and fled.

'Good God!' swore Dev, dropping his paintbrush.
'Tell her to push off!'

Picturing this, Alicia giggled weakly. His anger,
even if it was more principal than personal, made her
feel a little better. She had come to the session a mass
of tension, all of which had come pouring out after a
skilful question or two.

Regretfully, she shook her head. 'I can't.'

He studied her, hands on hips, the painting forgotten.

'Anyway,' Alicia took a deep breath, 'since I'm so
inept and unattractive, she's going to help me find
the man I need to give my life meaning.' She spoke
self-mockingly—something she had picked up from
him.

'Hell!' he said disgustedly. He looked lean and
hard and capable of standing up against anyone,
with his hair falling in a stallion's forelock across his
forehead, his eyes emerald-sharp. 'Well, she can't
force you into marriage.'

Alicia laughed uncertainly. Dev made an exasperated sound and crossed over to the window where
Alicia sat. 'Alicia, you don't have to be afraid of your
aunt. She cannot force you to do anything you don't
want to.'

'But maybe she's right,' Alicia murmured. 'Why
am I fighting it? Life would be a lot simpler their
way.'

'Is that what you want?'

'I don't know! They're happy!'

He shook his head. 'Because they're doing what they want. You would just be conforming.'

Alicia sighed. It was easy for Dev Rafferty to think that way. He didn't need anybody or anything. She couldn't imagine Dev Rafferty ever acting under duress. Turning back to the window forlornly, she felt Dev drop his hands on her shoulders. He shook her gently.

'Snap out of it, kid.' His hold was warm and comforting, but it was much as he would deal with an emotional child: brisk but kindly.

'I'm not a kid,' Alicia said tautly, turning to meet his frank green eyes. They narrowed slightly.

'No,' he agreed slowly. 'It's hard to tell quite what you are.'

'Well, whatever, I'm an unattractive one!' Alicia appended bitterly.

'What's the matter with you?' he inquired exasperatedly.

'Oh, they're right!' Alicia bit out frustratedly. 'Who would want me? Without the Carrington millions, I mean!'

'Plenty of men.' He smoothed her shoulders absently. 'You're an attractive girl.'

'Really?' she said drily. 'Do you find me attractive?'

'Of course,' he answered simply, his eyes direct.

Alicia swallowed, her lashes fluttering disbelievingly. His hand rose and brushed her hair back from her cheek.

'Very,' he murmured. Slowly his head bent and his cool, firm lips touched Alicia's astonished ones in a sweetly slow kiss. When he raised his head Alicia's heart was pounding crazily. She stared up at him, her thoughts erratic.

No one had ever kissed her that way before, as though she were a desirable woman. Certainly no one like Dev had ever tried. The brief but intense kiss fitted perfectly with all Alicia's notions of true love.

Dev was watching her, smiling faintly, assessingly, like a doctor judging a patient's progress.

'Dev!' she gasped with the impact of her unexpected idea. 'Do you love me?'

'Love?' His hands slid away from her shoulders, his face growing wary. 'Love is a word that covers a lot of ground.'

'Love' was not a word he would use lightly, she knew instinctively. But it was also a word Alicia was starved of hearing.

'Love,' she repeated stubbornly, almost as though she could force him to feel it by show of will.

'I care about you,' he said cautiously, taking in the desperate eagerness of her features. It was the same thing, she decided.

'Do you care about me enough to marry me?' she pressed boldly, catching his hand, like a child begging for attention.

'Wh—what?' he almost sounded alarmed.

'If you love me—' Alicia began.

'Alicia, I don't—' he broke off.

'Don't what?' she asked, trying to smile bravely. 'You just said you did care about me. Well? Don't you care enough?'

'I *do* care—' he stopped again, at a loss.

'And I love you,' she said steadily. 'I have from the first.'

He gave a sort of wince, his hands going out to her impulsively.

'Aunt Elizabeth wants me to marry,' Alicia added.

'I don't think I'm quite what Aunt Elizabeth had in mind,' Dev said grimly.

'You're what I had in mind.'

'But we barely know each other.' He was striving to sound amused and reasonable.

'We know we love each other.' She waited a long moment before adding softly, 'Don't we?'

His mouth opened. He took in her face slowly: the quiet confidence in her wide blue eyes, the smiling unsteadiness of her sensitive mouth.

'Uh—yes,' he said in a funny tone.

'Did you love Magda?' she asked suddenly.

'No.'

'I wouldn't be possessive,' she told him suddenly, as though struck by an idea. 'I think married people should keep their freedom. I want mine. And I know you're used to a different sort of life from the one I have led, but that's fine! I'm sick of my life. I like yours much better.' She hesitated, gauging his silence. 'I wouldn't—you know, expect you to spend all your time with me. You'd have just as much freedom as you do now—nearly.' She blushed. To her amazement he reddened too, faintly.

'It would even be good for your painting,' she rushed past the awkward moment. 'You'd be able to travel and have a house with a big studio—everything you wanted.'

'You don't have to sell me on marrying you,' he said roughly, looking away.

Alicia swallowed, saying very softly, afraid to hurt his pride. 'Is it the money?'

He glanced at her, his eyes very green. 'No, it's not,' he said shortly.

'Then what?' Alicia asked reasonably. 'If it's not

the money, and I promise it won't be your freedom—
and you love me . . . ?'

He continued to stare at her, suddenly cool and
withdrawn, his eyes unreadable.

'*Do* you love me?' Alicia questioned once more,
again afraid of his stillness.

'I love you.' Dev's voice faded away and he
seemed to listen to its echo with a kind of disbelief.
He repeated recklessly. 'Yes, I love you.'

'Then why don't you want to marry me?'

His eyes flickered. 'Tell me this, what would you
get out of this marriage?'

'You,' she said simply, and again his cheeks tinged
red.

'I'm no prize. What else?'

Alicia looked confused. 'What *else*? I—I suppose,'
she thought about it and said with sudden spirit, 'a
home of my own—our own—where I can do as I
please. I can finish University and get my degree. I'll
have freedom—*finally!*' Her eyes shone with excitement. 'With the money, I can do everything I've
wanted to for so long.' She looked up and her smile
dazzled. 'Best of all, I'll have you for my friend
and—' She couldn't quite finish it.

'Love?' he suggested kindly.

The images the word conjured sent the blood
churning through her veins. She couldn't meet his
eyes. She nodded.

'Are you *sure* you want to marry me?' he questioned softly, raising her chin with his long, clever
fingers.

'Yes,' Alicia said, looking up, her eyes steadfast.
'Are you?'

The green eyes flickered. 'Oh yes.' He leaned
towards her and pressed his lips against hers, as

though he were stamping his seal on a bargain.

By the time Alicia reached Carrington House, her happy daze began to give ground to nerves. Her spirits were not raised by the sight of Jacqueline's and Victor's Rolls parked in the front drive. She remembered guiltily that her sister and brother-in-law were dining at the house that night. Bravely, she decided it was just as well. She could get it out all at once.

Running late already, she hurried upstairs and changed her dress, reaching the drawing room to find the others sipping drinks and conversing quietly. They looked up in unison as Alicia entered.

'Alicia. At last.' Aunt Elizabeth greeted her coolly as Victor Smith-Lawes rose politely to his feet. He was a big man, tall and heavily built, in his early forties. His hair was fair, his eyes pale and blue, his skin had a ruddy quality that reminded Alicia of good beef. His personality was much like his appearance: heavy, prosperous. Alicia tried to like Victor but she resented his patronising manner. Fortunately he adored Jacqueline, and it was about the only good quality Alicia accepted in him.

She kissed Victor lightly, circling the back of the brocade-covered sofa to Jacqueline who raised her cheek for a sisterly peck. Jacqueline looked as lovely as ever in a black sheath that played up the porcelain whiteness of her skin. 'Hullo, Alicia,' she murmured. 'What kept you?'

'I'm about to tell you,' Alicia said. To her own ears she sounded self-important, stilted, formal. Awkwardly she crossed to Aunt Elizabeth who sat, regally erect, in her grey tweed skirt and white silk blouse.

'What do you mean, Alicia?' she asked, as Alicia

bent and kissed her scented cheek. At her tone, Alicia straightened, standing before them with hands clasped.

'I'm going to be married,' she said clearly. There was a crashing silence.

Beneath her powder Aunt Elizabeth paled, her knuckles gripping her cane so that the blue veins rose. Jacqueline and Victor's faces wore twin expressions of aghast astonishment. For several long seconds no one said anything, staring at the tall, thin girl they had never seen before.

Then, 'What do you *mean*?' Aunt Elizabeth demanded fiercely, and the other three turned, staring at her. At the harsh tone, Alicia forgot her resolve to be calm and reasonable, saying jerkily, 'That I'm going to be married! Some time this month.' She added at random into the appalled void, 'So you'll be able to go on your Caribbean cruise, after all.'

'But who?' Jacqueline asked blankly. 'Who do you *know* well enough to marry?' Alicia's chin jerked up defensively.

'He's an artist.' Aunt Elizabeth's eyes shut briefly, in agony. 'He's been painting my portrait for a month now. His name is Devereaux Rafferty.'

'A *month*,' Jacqueline demanded. 'You've only known him a month?'

At the same time Victor said crisply, 'Never heard of him.'

'I'd met him before that. At parties and exhibitions,' Alicia spoke staunchly, stretching the exact truth a little.

'Who-is-this-man?' Aunt Elizabeth bit out. She looked to Victor who shrugged helplessly.

'I've told you, his name is—'

'Who is his family? Where is he from? We know

nothing about him!' Angry colour flooded back to her aunt's face.

'*I* know about him.' Alicia tried to speak quietly, but her voice lacked authority, she felt. 'That's all that matters: he's thirty-four, eleven years older than me—Victor is fourteen years older than Jacqueline.' She was throwing out red herrings, but her family would not be detoured.

'Victor is not a nobody from nowhere!' snapped Jacqueline, and Victor nodded.

'Neither is Dev! I know about his background. He had parents—perfectly legitimate ones. What *you* mean is that he isn't rich. And you're right! But he isn't a fortune-hunter. He didn't even want to marry me at first.'

'Marvellous!' Aunt Elizabeth shaded her eyes with an unsteady hand. She seemed to have shrunk in size, withered.

Alicia said unsteadily, with an effort, 'He loves me, but he didn't want to marry me—because he knew this would be people's reaction.'

'He managed to put his qualms aside quickly enough,' Victor said heavily.

'I persuaded him,' Alicia said hotly. It was too difficult to stay calm and reasonable while they spoke about Dev like that. The urge was growing to scream that they had robbed her of everything else, they weren't going to deny her her future. Her nails dug into her hand with the effort to stay rational. She would gain nothing by hysteria.

'If he is so honest and above-board,' Aunt Elizabeth said in a dragging voice, 'why haven't we met him? Why isn't he here now?'

'We didn't realise we were in love until today. And he would have come with me, but I didn't want him to. I *knew* you would react like this,' Alicia added bitterly.

'Do you wonder? We didn't even know you were having your portrait painted,' Jacqueline exclaimed. Victor nodded as though she had struck at the heart of the matter.

'It was for Aunt Elizabeth's birthday,' Alicia said stiffly. 'It was a surprise.'

'No,' Aunt Elizabeth said, her voice shaking and acid, 'it is no surprise. I have always known you would do this to me.' Her face twisted. 'I can't bear to *look* at you,' she said in a voice of loathing.

Jacqueline and Victor looked faintly shocked at the venom in this outcry, and exchanged a look. The blood drained from Alicia's face. Slowly she turned, blindly crossing the hall, her heels tapping the gleaming surface, echoing emptily. She reached the staircase, stumbling up to her bedroom on unsteady legs. She reached the bed and collapsed on it, shaking with dry, angry sobs. The darkness seemed to cling, shielding her, and Alicia pressed her hands to her face, reliving the scene downstairs. She started to cry, then stopped herself. She would not let them make her shed any tears over marrying Dev.

If they made her choose between them, she *would*—and with less difficulty than they realised. Not from *them* had she received tenderness or patience or humour. She thought of Dev with a surge of passionate gratitude, of near adoration. He was so brilliant and talented and *beautiful*, yet he loved *her*, the individual Alicia.

CHAPTER FOUR

LONG after she heard Jacqueline and Victor drive away, Alicia lay awake and listening in the still, dark house. Vaguely she wondered what she could tell Dev about this evening. If Aunt Elizabeth banished her then she would have to tell him the truth, but if Aunt Elizabeth decided to put up a front, perhaps she could smooth over everything. She was afraid, for reasons she didn't analyse, that her family's disapproval might somehow sway Dev, change his mind— for her sake. The thought terrified her. She sat up in bed. He couldn't abandon her now. Her life would be sheer hell. He had to stand by her, help her escape.

The choice of words, the direction of her thoughts, suddenly amused Alicia. She lay back down. Of course he would stand by her. He loved her. Why should that change? The thought of his love was vastly comforting, like being held and rocked. She fastened on the idea and slowly drifted into peaceful sleep.

Aunt Elizabeth made her attitude known at breakfast the next morning. She was immaculate but haggard, her early appearance at the table making Alicia suspect that her aunt had not slept the night before. The formidable lady winced at the sight of food, sipping her black coffee with the air of one focusing her energies on a terrible task.

'You are quite serious about marrying this man?' she questioned into the silence as Alicia was finishing her cereal.

Alicia started slightly and nodded, avoiding her aunt's eyes.

'Then you had better bring him home and formally introduce him, hadn't you? It is best to put as fine a face on this as we can.' Her tone was bitter. Who was the face for, Alicia wondered.

'We will have him to dinner Friday evening,' Aunt Elizabeth continued coldly. 'You may discuss the menu with Cook.'

Alicia nodded again. She didn't dare argue when her aunt was being this accommodating—she had expected the 'do not darken my doorstep' speech. Her relief surprised her. Even now, did it matter so much what her family did?

'What arrangements have you made?' Aunt Elizabeth inquired reluctantly.

'We hadn't got that far,' Alicia admitted.

'I will be happy to advise you,' her aunt said, and the irony in that made Alicia flush.

'Thank you,' she muttered.

Aunt Elizabeth's smile was acrid. 'I'm sure this— Rafferty will have his own ideas,' was all she said. There was something in her tone that made Alicia uneasy, and more unsettling, there was a kind of pity for her in Aunt Elizabeth's pale eyes.

On the weekend they began hunting for a house to move into. It was fun as she walked with Dev through empty houses, listening to his half-joking comments on possible owners past and present. Alicia wondered if she could be in a slight state of shock since it was so hard not to laugh hysterically when estate agents started discussing personal tastes and 'suiting needs'.

She wondered if she and Dev *looked* like a couple.

Maybe when she had a ring on her finger, Alicia decided, something tangible to look at and touch, maybe then she would *feel* it.

They didn't know a thing about each other, she thought vaguely, watching Dev assessing a room for a potential studio. But then she reminded herself quickly that they knew all they needed to. The rest would come with time. They would grow old together and know each other inside out. Twenty years from now she would look back and marvel that now she couldn't even tell if he was happy.

They found the house Sunday afternoon. Alicia had begun to give up hope. It didn't matter to her what the house was like as long as Dev thought it was perfect. But Dev, it transpired, thought very few things in life perfect. Light, she deduced finally, was the key. The sun had to be on the proper sides of the house at the proper times. It never seemed to be—at least not in the houses that had stables—Alicia's prerequisite. By Sunday afternoon she had stopped giggling and her feet had begun hurting. And then, they found it—like paradise after purgatory: a lovely house, big and gracious, entering a comfortable middle-age. It was in a wealthy section of the outer suburbs, rather secluded. There were stables, a pool and lots of rooms for lots of future children—a subject the estate agents tended to bring up. The lighting was perfect and Dev could take half the top floor for his studio. With a little renovating and decorating it would be perfect by the time they returned from their honeymoon.

They signed the necessary papers and went out to dinner to celebrate. It was, Alicia realised, suddenly nervous, their first real 'date'. She kept looking to Dev for her cue. But Dev was, for once, unresponsive to her plight. It was as though without a third person to remind him of his fiancée's presence he completely forgot her. Or not forgot so much, as relegated her to the place of a background fixture, as though she were a child a weary adult could rely on to entertain itself.

'So,' Alicia said at random, to talk herself away from uncomfortable thoughts. 'So—'

'So?' Dev's eyes widened slowly. They looked dark in the soft light.

'Can you make it Friday?' Alicia inquired politely.

'Of course.'

There was no 'of course' about it as far as Alicia could see. He had been non-committal yesterday morning when she had broached the subject.

'Aunt Elizabeth will want to know all our wedding plans.' Her tone was falsely light, and she was increasingly tense. In the shadows his face had a remote look. She didn't like his smile, either, as she felt that he was laughing at her, somehow. 'Where we're honeymooning—' Alicia bit out, clattering her fork against her clean plate.

'Where would you like to go?' Dev asked quietly, his eyes on her fidgeting hands. She stilled them, shrugging.

'You're the expert.'

'At what?' He *was* laughing at her, his eyes tilted with private amusement.

Alicia's chin lifted proudly, her eyes met his, daring him to laugh openly. Nobody laughed at a Carrington. Her taut face took the humour out of his. He said quite gently, it could have been a warning:

'It's not too late to call it off.'

'Do you want to?'

'No.'

Alicia's heart resumed beating. 'Neither do I.' She

nearly choked out the words. For a moment there . . .
To cover her terror, her weak relief, she said, 'I don't
care where we go. Maybe a beach somewhere.' She
remembered his telling her how much he enjoyed
swimming when he lived in Greece.

'Any particular beach?' He was smiling again.
'France? The Virgin Islands? Hawaii?'

'Hawaii,' she decided at random.

'I've never been there. It should be interesting.'
He looked past her to the approaching waiter.

Alicia gulped down her wine.

The following week the engagement was announced
in the society pages, and all the polite world shook its
head in sorry comprehension and sent gifts. Among
Dev's circle of acquaintances Alicia sensed a sceptic-
al acceptance. It was very obvious what everyone
thought. Alicia was startled to find within herself a
well of offended hostility. It was insulting to Dev and
it was insulting to her. She planned (and her family
was obviously relieved to comply) a small, private
wedding. Dev left the arrangements to her. He
seemed almost, at times, merely to be drifting with
the tide rather than being an active participant.
Alicia didn't mind. She couldn't see Dev poring over
silver patterns or picking china. She *was* a little
surprised that there was no noticeable change in his
behaviour towards her. They had been engaged for
over a week, but his kisses remained brief, his attitude teasing.

On Friday evening Dev came to dinner at Carrington House to, as Aunt Elizabeth sarcastically
put it, celebrate the nuptials. Jacqueline and Victor,
the only guests, arrived early to bolster Aunt Elizabeth's morale, while upstairs Alicia changed

clothes five times hoping to find something to bolster *her* morale. She kept one ear cocked for sounds of Dev's advent. She wanted to be first to greet him—suddenly, ridiculously, she felt protective of him. She knew only too well how her family could be.

She had just finished dressing, having finally settled on a grey tweed skirt and white linen blouse—at least she felt authoritative—when she heard his car in the drive below and hurried down to the front door, just beating the butler, Walters.

'I'll get it,' she gasped, practically sliding to a stop. Walters cocked a supercilious brow and withdrew. Alicia turned and opened the door. 'Hi!' she said breathlessly, her stomach fluttering butterflies.

He looked surprisingly formal in a grey flannel suit and grey pinstripe shirt. She had never seen him in a suit before. It threw her. 'We match!' she added, and he laughed, handing her the wrapped portrait, completed two days before, for Aunt Elizabeth.

'You look nice.' He dropped a light kiss on the tip of her nose. Conscious of the open drawing room door behind them, Alicia tried awkwardly to return it. She felt a little surge of pride, studying his elegantly suited height, that he belonged to her.

'They're all in there,' she whispered, her fingers closing on the painting frame. She didn't have anything to be ashamed of, and he certainly didn't look worried about meeting the Carringtons; all the same she dreaded saying, 'Shall we go in?' It came out nervously—she had known it would.

He smiled, his tilted eyes taking in her forced casualness. His hand lifted and slid behind her head, drawing her near, tilting her face up to his. His head bent and his lips touched her parted ones in a long warm kiss. When he released her, Alicia gasped a little, her heart pounding, her legs trembling. His eyes crinkled at her bemusement.

'Let's,' he agreed. There was something bracing about this treatment, Alicia decided, returning his smile.

She turned, leading the way back to the drawing room. She barely hesitated on the threshold, walking briskly in and saying bravely, 'I'd like you all to meet Dev.'

They had certainly heard the front door, but from the silence they might have all been caught completely by surprise. Alicia was hotly aware of those brief seconds' scrutiny before Aunt Elizabeth said frostily, 'How do you do, Mr Rafferty?' and Victor rose to his feet. Jacqueline offered a sweet cold smile from her corner of the sofa.

'Miss Carrington.' Dev approached Aunt Elizabeth, and briefly took the hand she cursorily offered. He shook hands with Victor and nodded to Jacqueline who nodded graciously back.

'Please sit down, Mr Rafferty,' Aunt Elizabeth instructed.

Dev complied. Alicia thought how incongruous he looked in the cream-coloured brocade chair: so alert and vital. Even his hair colour seemed too alive for the quiet stately room. Alicia leaned against the back of his chair and Aunt Elizabeth said impatiently, 'Do stop hovering, Alicia. Sit down.'

Alicia obeyed, dropping on to the sofa beside Jacqueline, hearing Dev say, faintly sardonic, 'It was so kind of you to invite me, Miss Carrington.' She gave him a nervous glance.

'Hardly,' Aunt Elizabeth returned.

Jacqueline interpolated smoothly, 'You're an artist, Devereaux?'

He turned his very green gaze in her direction, taking in her pure, chiselled features.

'Dev brought the portrait, Aunt Elizabeth,' Alicia put in eagerly, rising and bringing the portrait out from behind Dev's chair where she had propped it. She carried it across to her aunt who took it reluctantly. Alicia gave Dev a hopeful look, but his expression was impassive.

'How exciting,' murmured Jacqueline.

'How is the art business these days?' Victor inquired, as Aunt Elizabeth unwrapped the portrait.

'Steadily improving,' Dev replied, again with that cynical tone Alicia distrusted. She foresaw a night of this back and forth sniping, and cringed inwardly.

'What will you have to drink?' Victor inquired, going over to the drinks' trolley. 'Scotch?'

'White wine.' It hung in the air like a proclamation. Victor nearly winced. *Real* men, in Victor's opinion, did not drink anything but spirits.

Aunt Elizabeth tore away the last of the wrapping paper and the portrait stood revealed to her. After a long moment she said in a brittle tone:

'You are a clever man, Mr Rafferty.'

Jacqueline rose and moved to where she could view the painting. Her brows rose delicately. 'That's really excellent! Victor, come and see.'

Victor wandered over and Alicia exchanged a look with Dev. His expression cleared a little and he gave her a faintly malicious grin. She found herself smiling back, reassured.

'First rate,' Victor opined generously.

'Yes, thank you,' Aunt Elizabeth said without pleasure, staring down at Alicia's painted features.

'Dinner is served,' Walters announced from the dining room doorway.

Together they rose and went into dinner, Dev and Alicia moving with Jacqueline, while Victor solicitously escorted Aunt Elizabeth.

Although the meal was superb, it could have been paper wads for all the attention Alicia paid. Aunt Elizabeth was barely icily polite, Jacqueline consciously enchanting and Victor condescending. Dev treated them with an ironic courtesy that did not quite cover that he despised them; despised their patent snobbery and even more their pretence of cordiality. The Carringtons so obviously deplored Alicia's choice, and so obviously were putting up a front to hide their appalled feelings. As dinner progressed to the strawberries and cream dessert, Alicia's shame grew. She could see her family so clearly through Rafferty's direct, piercing gaze.

'Of course I can see why you'd rather not bother with a big wedding,' Jacqueline was saying pensively, licking a smidge of cream from her upper lip with her small pink tongue. 'I remember *our* wedding.' She gave Victor a long, languid look. 'The fuss, the bother, the publicity with all the magazines.' She sighed. 'It was perfect.'

Down to the last diamond in her ring, Alicia reflected. She looked down at her own beringed hand. Dev had chosen the ring. It was an odd design: heavy, twisted gold, like brambles, entwined with tiny diamonds. Although it was barbaric in design, it suited Alicia's long, capable, brown hands. Jacqueline caught the direction of Alicia's stare and said meaningfully, 'You have *unusual* taste, Devereaux.'

He quirked his brows, retorting casually, 'Another term for a sophisticated palate?'

'I'm sure of that.' She gave him her charming, pointed smile, casting Alicia an elder sister look.

'They say it's the more jaded palate which seeks the fresh and unspoiled, and vice versa.'

Aunt Elizabeth said sharply, 'I assume you have been to see Mr Ellis?'

Mr Ellis of Ellis, Ellis, Ellis and Farraday, was the family solicitor. Alicia and Dev had been that week to make their wills and remove the restrictions of Alicia's inheritance in order to buy their new house. Alicia had half-dreaded the encounter, but they had met nothing but professional courtesy and congratulations on their betrothal.

'Yes,' Alicia answered. She could follow the thoughts behind her aunt's expressionless mask.

'You'll want to make some smart investment decisions now,' Victor commented, forking a large, fat strawberry into his mouth.

'I'm sure Mr Rafferty has his own ideas about investment,' Aunt Elizabeth said.

'Art investment can be a risky business,' Victor went on, unclued to Aunt Elizabeth's tone. 'Of course you must know a bit about that.'

'I don't intend to interfere with Alicia's plans for her capital.'

'But I'm sure you have an excellent head for business,' Jacqueline murmured, and Dev gave her an ironic look.

Alicia thought of the inscription she was going to have etched in his wedding band: 'Love's Good Fortune.' *Because it's my good fortune to love you*, Alicia mentally answered his imagined inquiry. She couldn't help what people thought, but she would make it up to him as best she could. Already she was full of plans. For his wedding present she had bought him a tall, leggy grey hunter, so they could ride together. She had a million projects for the house.

She couldn't wait till they were married. She couldn't wait till this evening was over.

When it finally was over, she walked out with Dev to his car. It was a cold, crisp night, the dark sky smeared with stars, almost wavering in their distant intensity.

'I'm sorry,' she said into the silence, broken only by their feet on the stone court.

'For what? Because they don't like me? Forget it. I don't like them.' He laughed, not unkindly, at her unhappy look. 'Don't worry. We'll all manage to get along for your sake.' He gave her another light kiss and withdrew his arm from around her shoulders. She immediately missed its warm weight. She wished she could go home with him then and there, but knew she was being childish.

'Jacqueline's very beautiful though, isn't she?' she asked suddenly. Jacqueline had been very lovely and very captivating in a cutting way that night.

He laughed shortly, without particular niceness. 'Rather typical I think.'

Alicia's heart warmed with unsisterly pleasure. 'I'm not like them,' she said abruptly.

'No.' His expression softened slightly. 'It will be a pleasure to take you out of their hands.'

He sounded more like someone fighting a custody battle than a fiancé, Alicia recognised wryly. She shrugged the thought aside, reluctantly releasing his hand as he got into the black Ferrari.

Alicia's wedding day dawned sunny and cold, mist evaporating as though punctured on the spires of the numerous London churches. She dressed with Jacqueline's help and her stomach churned, her fingers trembling as she slipped into the calf-length, white silk dress. Her reflection in the mirror seemed out of focus, her face almost tight with nerves beneath the sheer veil. The dress looked a little like a Victorian schoolgirl smock, but, according to Jacqueline, it suited Alicia's simplicity—which could have meant anything.

The drive took a scant few minutes in the car, silence only lifted by Jacqueline's forced cheer. Aunt Elizabeth sat erect and grim, contained. Before she had time to register it, Alicia was walking down the aisle, looking into Dev's strangely grave eyes, repeating her vows and—married!

The reception passed in a blur of congratulations and rice. She was only conscious of Dev. Every time she looked at him he was watching her, his eyes without laughter, his face quiet. He looked, she reflected, sipping her champagne, like one of the stone angels from the church: beautiful, meditative and compassionate. She found she didn't care much for the idea.

It was a relief to leave for the airport, except that then Alicia was alone with this suddenly reserved, taciturn stranger. She couldn't think of anything to say to him. It was terrible. They sat on the plane and Dev drank while Alicia pretended to sleep. Frantically she wondered what was wrong? It was so *stupid* to feel shy of Dev. But he wasn't like Dev. They had been closer when they were just friends. At least they had *talked*. She had married a stranger. It was a mistake. She should have listened to Aunt Elizabeth. What in God's name could they talk about for a whole week . . . ? On and on wound Alicia's panicked meditations, as the hours flew by.

The plane landing, Customs, the brief ride to the hotel, all passed with alarming swiftness. One by one all possible delays fell: the hotel check-in, the elevator ride, tipping the bell-boy—

Behind the bell-boy, Dev shut the door to their suite and turned, leaning against it, facing Alicia. She stood, surrounded by their luggage, looking back with wide, blue eyes.

'Well, Mrs Rafferty?' he inquired.

'Well?' She lifted her chin. Out of her depth maybe, but she was still a Carrington.

'It's rather late. Shall I order room service?'

'Oh, I don't think I could eat,' Alicia told him, then winced at her rejection of a perfectly good stall. 'I think I'll have a shower,' she added hastily.

He nodded and picked his suitcase up, tossing it on the foot of the king-sized bed. 'Which side of the bed do you prefer?' He sounded very formal.

She blinked. 'Er—it doesn't matter.'

'All right. You take the left.' He began to unpack, apparently down to business. Alicia followed his example, unpacked, hung her clothes up and went into the shower. She took as long as she dared, finally dressing slowly in the cream silk peignoir set Jacqueline had given her.

She stepped out into the suite. It was nearly dark, a ribbon of orange streaming through the dark sky above the darker ocean. Dev was seated on the terrace watching the beach below where a brown boy ran along the hotel wharf lighting tiki torches. He had ordered tall, fruity drinks adorned with pineapple.

While Dev had his turn in the shower, Alicia sat sipping her drink, the balmy evening air caressing her bare skin. The alcohol calmed her jittery nerves, counteracting emotional and physical exhaustion of the day. She began to wish Dev would come. It seemed she had spent half her life on the night-darkened balcony listening to faint music waft up from the hotel bar.

She heard the bathroom door open, heard his feet pad quietly across the carpeted floor to the verandah doors. She felt him behind her and her heart began to race again. Her mouth dried as he bent and kissed her bare shoulder. He smelt soap-clean, his hair still damp. She shivered at the velvety touch of his mouth trailing over her skin. In the dark he was a white shadow, but his touch was breath-stoppingly real. She shut her eyes, feeling that her fate was out of her hands and heard his murmured question:

'Alicia?'

CHAPTER FIVE

A QUIVER of anticipation feathered down Alicia's spine. She turned her head and Dev's nuzzling lips met hers in a slow, intoxicating kiss. Alicia's heart jerked and began to pound in heavy thuds. She felt his arm slip behind her cool, bare shoulders, and as though directed by a separate will, her arms rose, slipping about his neck. Sliding his other arm beneath, Dev scooped her up with an easy grace, moving with her into the moonlit room. It was like a scene from an old romantic movie, Alicia thought hazily, cradled against the smooth material robing his chest.

Dev settled her on the bed and lay down beside her. Alicia was glad of the darkness. She was afraid to look at him. Her body felt hot and trembling; she was frightened and impassioned at the same time. Then came the hysterical desire to laugh. He was so smooth, so *practised*. His fingers were at the fine lace straps that fastened her nightgown; they fell free and she felt the gown gliding away.

Dark or not, an instinctive flood of embarrassment washed over her. 'Do we have to take *all* our clothes off?' she whispered into the darkness.

His hands stopped. There was a long moment of silence. Then Dev's head dropped against her arm and she could feel him shaking soundlessly.

'Dev?' she asked alarmed, raising her head. He rolled aside and the bed vibrated with the increased force of his shaking.

'Dev! What are you *laughing* at?' she exclaimed, amazed. It was the last thing in the world she had expected. She fought the nervous desire to giggle.

'You,' he gulped helplessly. His tremors lessened gradually and he took a deep breath. 'Oh lord,' he sighed. He rolled on to his side, studying her, head propped on his elbow. She tried to read his face in the silvery shadows.

'What should I do?' she asked, wanting to help.

'Don't,' he pleaded shakily. For an exasperated moment she thought he was going to go off again, but he took another long breath, saying 'All right,' so determinedly that Alicia swallowed. She had not thought much about the actual wedding night—the very idea made her wince in anticipation of her awkward naïvety revealed—but Dev, incapacitated with laughter, had never entered her brain. She wasn't sure she liked this version.

Almost absently he began to play with her hand, tickling her palm and stroking the soft inside of her wrist with his thumb. 'You know, I don't deserve this,' he said softly.

'Deserve what?' Her voice sounded like a polite child's, but the little chills the feathery brush of his fingers raised on her skin, were not a childish response.

'This—innocence,' he said with sudden difficulty. His hand slid up her arm and he stroked with his thumb her long, slender throat. 'You are so *young*,' he muttered, bending over her. His lips found hers, parting them with gentle insistence. His body was heavy against hers. She could feel his smooth warmth through the thin silk of her gown. His robe was gone, she noted with vague surprise, and hers was going fast.

With an effort, she directed her thoughts away from his touch, wondering whether he actually minded her being so coltishly awkward. She supposed there had been an awful lot of women before her. Dev's hands cupped her breast and she stiffened as she felt his lips on her nipple. Alicia gasped, frantically trying to think. *I should have read something*, she realised, her brain harassed with sensation. *I don't know what's happening.*

'So sweet,' murmured Dev. His hair felt like rough, damp silk against her skin, his body taut and hard and very male.

Didn't know what was happening? She knew all right, and it scared her to death. He was touching her everywhere, his hands patient and caressing. She couldn't escape his intimate fingers, moving, stroking, tantalising; prying into her very mind. Everywhere he touched felt hot and throbbing, alive to contact. Her entire body felt strung tight and quivering. It was hard to keep quiet, to lie still and calm. Her body seemed to be moving of its own volition in response to his.

When he finally lowered himself on to her, a shock went through Alicia that was partly pain, partly fierce satisfaction. Then they were locked together, one, and the intimacy was almost more than she could bear. She hadn't expected this total vulnerability, total abandon of control as they clung together. All barriers were down before the desperate urgency moving her. There was a moment of intense pain, then warm, flooding fulfilment. Through half-shut eyes she saw Dev's face blind and shuddering with an agony of pleasure. His weight collapsed on to her, his breathing ragged. She could hear his heart hammering in her ear.

Whatever she had felt, he had felt ten times more acutely, she realised. Wondering, she moved her hands over his ribs and lower back. His skin felt damp. This was what the books and movies raved about. This was what she had wanted, what she had searched for with blind insistence. She had never felt so close to another person. She didn't want the feeling of satisfied unity to end, yet it was not as she had imagined it. It was hard to determine why. Somehow she felt a little detached about it all.

After long minutes he moved from her, whispering, 'Did I hurt you? I'm sorry.' His arm slid under, pulling her close. He kissed her, his mouth warm and lingering.

'Is that how it's supposed to be?' Beyond the feeling of weakness, of being pleasurably drained, she was unexpectedly a little sore.

'I guess the first time hurts a little. Next time will be better,' he reassured, sounding drowsy. He rubbed his cheek against her hair.

'Like riding?' Alicia suggested.

'Mm.' The idea seemed to amuse him. A minute or two later, she could tell by his stillness and the even tone of his breathing that he slept. Without his conscious presence the room felt lonely, foreign. Alicia nestled against Dev and also fell asleep.

She woke to a slow awareness of sensation, of his hands once more searching and caressing. Half awake, feeling stiff and sore, Alicia murmured protestingly. His lips silenced hers as he continued to touch. His slow, deliberate hands were painstakingly building a fire within her. Alicia could not control the response that flamed to life within her. She began to move, her body restless and aching with instinctive desire. She wanted him *now*. From a frustrating distance she heard Dev's low, amused laugh. His fingers teased.

He held back, watching her grow more frustrated. She reached for him. 'Not yet,' he said softly. His hands were driving her frantic. Alicia groaned, unable to control her body's arch. Her hands pulled at him, and to Alicia's intense relief he came, with satisfying hardness. A rough little cry of gladness broke from her. She couldn't breathe or see, only feel the driving ecstasy. Then the night seemed to split apart, bright with white-hot passion. Alicia felt as though she were spinning, lost in a vortex, with only Dev's voice in her ear to anchor her to reality.

In the aftermath, holding each other gently, Alicia finally understood.

Alicia lay basking in bright afternoon sunshine. From the bathroom she could hear the muffled sound of the shower and Dev's cheerful whistling. She smiled, stretching luxuriously against the pillows.

The bathroom door opened and Dev stepped out, towelling his head.

'Hey, we've only got a week,' he teased, and Alicia grinned languidly.

'Shall I order breakfast?' she asked, reaching for the phone.

'You mean lunch, I think. It's after noon.'

They looked at each other smiling with a kind of unspoken satisfaction. Dev glanced away first, saying briskly, 'Come on girl. Let's get down to the beach before the sun sets.'

'What happens when the sun sets?' she inquired innocently.

His look was exaggeratedly lustful before he returned to the bathroom, leaving Alicia chuckling.

She threw aside the bedcovers and dived through her chaotic suitcases, triumphantly pulling forth her swimsuit.

She wished later, examining herself in the suite mirror, that it was a more attractive suit. It was a practical black one-piece, and she looked a little pale for Hawaii in it.

'Dev?' she questioned, frowning at her reflection. 'What do you know about make-up?'

'Never wear it. Makes me break out.' He grinned at her raised eyes.

'I mean, do you know anything about applying it? I have all these—' she gestured at the tubes, bottles, compacts and colourful jars littering the dressing-table top, 'but I don't know how to apply it correctly.'

'Hmm.' He rose and handed her a tube from the pile. 'Try this, it's the right tone.' She examined the red-brown gel doubtfully. 'That and mascara. You don't want a lot of junk on your face when we're swimming.'

'I just don't want to let you down,' Alicia replied absently, uncapping the tube.

'Would you stop it!' Dev said sharply, and she looked up surprised. 'It makes me feel terrible when you talk as though I were some sort of—of paragon.'

'I only meant—' Alicia swallowed nervously '—that you're used to such beautiful, sophisticated women. I want you to find me attractive—'

'I do. I always have.'

'Oh, I know I'm *interesting*-looking,' Alicia assured hastily. 'But I want you to think I'm pretty, too—as a woman not just as a *subject*.'

'Are you nuts?' he inquired. 'How could I find you pretty as one and not the other?'

'You know what I *mean*,' Alicia said, herself now impatient. 'You might find someone attractive to paint, but not *personally* attractive. Magda was completely different from me.'

'You'll notice I didn't marry Magda.'

'No, but she's still somebody you—loved. You found her attractive. Well, how could you find me attractive, then? She's small and beautiful and— endowed. I'm built like a boy and plain.'

'You're not plain and you didn't *feel* to *me*, like a boy last night.' At the look in his green eyes, Alicia glanced away, confused. 'If you want to use cosmetics, go ahead. But don't change to please me. I like you fine just as you are.' He turned away restlessly.

In the end she settled for the blusher and waterproof mascara, and was pleased with the subtle change. Dev's comments affected her positively. After all, if Dev thought her attractive, what did what anyone else think matter? She walked beside him through the lobby, down the stairs and out to the beach feeling unusually confident. Her habitual slouch shrugged off without even noticing, her eyes met others steadily. Amazing what one day—and night—of marriage could accomplish, she reflected.

Even off-season, Hawaii was beautiful. Sunny and warm, the sky and ocean melted into one sweep of aching blue. They left busy, bustling Waikki to find an empty beach further down the coast: a cove of silky white sand secluded behind mossy, trailing vine-twisted rocks and stately palms.

They spread out their plush beach towels and while Dev slathered her over in coconut tanning oil, Alicia read aloud from the guide book she had picked up in the hotel, lobby.

'Do you know,' she informed Dev, as he massaged

the oil into her shoulders with strong, kneading movements, 'the only land mammal indigenous to the islands is a small bat?'

'No—I'm not even sure what indigenous means.'

'And,' Alicia continued, turning the page, 'there are over nine hundred species of flowering plants, more than three hundred of which are trees. We should go to the botanical gardens while we're here.'

'How many flowering species does Britain have?' Dev inquired curiously.

'I don't know.'

'Then how do you know that nine hundred is a lot?'

'I don't: I think it's just supposed to be a point of interest.'

'Does that book contain any really useful information,' Dev queried, handing her the tanning lotion, 'like where to find the best places to eat?'

'I've got another book for that,' Alicia remarked, laying aside the book and squirting the oil in her palm. She smoothed her hands over Dev's long, lean back, as he sat before her. He still wore his Levi's and a straw sun-hat with an exotically feathered band. Alicia felt like a drab little hen next to him. She supposed they didn't look like much of a couple—she so conservative and reserved. Then she brightened up. Conservative or not, it was she rubbing oil into his back. She got up on her knees and smoothed the lotion over his chest, her hands lingering. From the corner of her eye, she saw Dev's lips twitch humorously.

While Dev dozed, Alicia skimmed lazily through her book, glancing now and then over his recumbent body with the unconscious pleasure of possession. When they began to get hot they ran down to the

crystal-blue water, running and splashing in the
surf. When they tired of running up and down the
beach and cresting the breakers, they returned wet
and sandy to their towels, to dry.

The afternoon sped by and soon it was time to
return to the hotel for a shower and change before the
evening's luau. Alicia took a long shower, then
creamed herself with cool, moisturising lotion, and
dusted scented powder over that. When she went out
into the suite, she found Dev had ordered mai tais.
While he showered she drank hers, drying her hair in
a rumply mass of curls. Finally she pinned an orchid
Dev had bought on their return from the beach, in
her hair, and studied the result. She determined,
dusting blusher over her sun-warmed face, that the
results were nothing shabby. As soon as she could,
she wanted to get some really stunning clothes. It
was important to feel beautiful, she decided, when
one was married.

The luau was fun, although Alicia was drinking
more than usual and saw it through a happy haze of
alcohol and love. Above everything else she was
aware of Dev. She seemed to see the whole evening
through his eyes, rarely taking her gaze from his
torchlit face. She laughed when he laughed, made
her expression match his interested one. It amazed
her that he could lounge there so coolly casual while
every nerve cell in her body vibrated impatiently.

The entertainment seemed as endless as the meal
had done: A Don Ho clone singing island and modern love songs, then hula dancers. As the evening
progressed, the dancing grew less inhibited. The
wild rhythm of the native drums matched the increasingly feverish throb of Alicia's pulse. When Dev
glanced over at her during the show, she gave him a

wide, direct look of unmistakable meaning. His eyes
flickered and without haste or hesitation, he
gathered their things and moved her through the
crowd, his fingers cool and courteous on her elbow.
Alone in the elevator, he leaned back, grinning a grin
to match her own.

'What a shameless hussy I've married.'

'Wouldn't Aunt Elizabeth be shocked,' she
agreed.

The following morning they were up surprisingly
early, and after breakfast Alicia offered to go shop-
ping while Dev spent another day on the beach, but
to her relief he chose to go along with her. They went
to a number of small, expensive shops and Alicia
found that Dev had decided preferences in style and
colour. It was just as well, she reflected, since her
own taste was indifferent, her only intent, to please
him.

The exotic print shirts: parrots, flowers, trees,
shells and fish; the various coloured jeans: black, red,
white, khaki, indigo and olive; the cotton dresses in
dolphin, lizard, orchid and bird prints, and solid
brights; all these Alicia watched go into boxes and
bags with a feeling of delight.

The three evening gowns: a filmy black with a
raggedy handkerchief hemline, an indigo-blue strapless silk and a honey-gold, shimmering sheath with a
wrap bust, she watched with less certainty. They did
not look like her, she worried—although there was
no one else she could think of who they did look like.
She liked them better than she liked the gowns
Jacqueline had helped her pick for her trousseau—
those had all looked better on Jacqueline than Alicia.
She couldn't see Jacqueline in any of these; they were
too off-beat.

She flatly protested over a black wisp of bikini, a printed blue maillot and a red maillot.

'*Red?* I can't wear red!'

'Don't be stupid,' Dev said absently. To the sales-girl's surprise, Alicia blushed as though com-plimented—which in fact she had been.

In the privacy of the dressing room, Alicia turned and twisted, eyeing herself critically. The suit's cut gave her a long, leggy look and the colour worked well with her hair and skin. Although she refused to parade the results in the show room, she reluc-tantly agreed to buy the suits, and Dev seemed satis-fied.

But when Alicia told him gaily that it was his turn, he became difficult, refusing, telling her that he didn't want anything.

'But I *want* you to have something,' Alicia pro-tested with a touch of Carrington persistence. 'We've just bought me dozens of things. It's not fair.'

'I'd rather not.'

He wasn't looking at her and she said with sudden awareness, 'It's not the money is it? The money is yours now.'

'No.' He looked at her then.

'You *chauvinist!*' Alicia exclaimed. 'Of course it is! And I've got the papers to prove it!' His answering smile was faint, and she said tentatively, 'Dev, *you're* not worried about what *people* might think!'

'I don't care what anyone thinks,' he said roughly, adding as an afterthought, 'except you.'

'*I* think you need some new things,' Alicia said mischievously. His lips twitched but he shook his head, repeating slowly, 'I'd rather not.'

'Well, I want to buy you something,' Alicia in-sisted.

'You can buy me a new pair of sunglasses,' he said agreeably. 'I've just broken these.' He held them up ruefully.

They bought the sunglasses, then lunched in a Japanese restaurant with carp pools, served by girls in kimonos. Alicia quickly dismissed the incident of the money squabble, knowing better than to insist on anything with Dev. His behaviour was incomprehensible to her. She supposed he would sort out his feelings eventually. She didn't intend to go through the next fifty years with separate bank accounts.

Other than his sudden aversion to her money, Dev was becoming comfortably familiar to Alicia. She understood that he had a highly-strung artistic temperament and that his changing disposition did not reflect on her personally. She knew that it was a compliment to her that he was so relaxed and receptive with her.

He was in many ways a cynic, and he had experienced many things, pleasant and unpleasant, that she never would—nor want to—but his cynicism never touched her. With Alicia he was invariably indulgent—though sometimes distant. She knew she amused him, but it was a tender amusement. He thought her very naïve; she guessed she was, but she knew one or two things about him instinctively. She knew that he had been lonely—even with Magda; even without recognising it—before their marriage. Lonely as she had been lonely: for a fellow spirit, a companion. She knew that his charm and self-mockery were a barrier, and that he never lowered that barrier, except occasionally with her—not even realising that he had done so. She knew that he was arrogant and not used to considering anyone else, so his attentiveness was all the more impressive—and his slips more forgivable. He was incredibly patient with her, and she was grateful.

The days flew by in golden days and velvet nights. Every day there was something new to do: a helicopter tour of the islands, the long scenic drive up Haleakala—'House of the Sun'—on Maui, deep-sea fishing, skin-diving in the coral reefs, museums, botanical gardens, sailboating or just swimming and sunning on a variety of beaches—including one with black sand and lush ferns. Alicia bought a camera, intending to give it to Dev, but at the last moment—knowing his touchiness about presents—not designating ownership. They took hundreds of dollars-worth of photographs; Dev devising arty shots, Alicia snapping everything—especially Dev—that came into focus.

Although in the day time he was indulgent and amused and patient—unintentionally reminding Alicia of the catching up she had to do—in the night there was nothing patronising in his manner. He enjoyed her, she realised, with a thrill of discovery. The knowledge gave her courage to reach out to him.

One night, towards the end of their honeymoon, she moved towards Dev instead of passively waiting for him to make the advances. She touched him tentatively and felt his surprise. She hesitated.

'Yes,' Dev said huskily. 'Yes, touch me.'

It was novel and sweet to hold him, touch him. It was gratifying to know that she was shaking and moving him as much as he did her. It gave her a heady sense of power, but in the aching sweetness of consummation there was no imbalance. Each night seemed more meltingly perfect than the last, yet in the back of Alicia's brain some insecurity persisted. Perhaps if she had not known his last lover it would have been easier to assure herself it was as beautiful for him as it was for her.

On their last night, as they rested drained and peaceful, Alicia asked Dev softly, 'How does this—compare?'

'Hmm?' He sounded sleepy. He was often drowsy afterwards, perhaps because of the release.

'How does this compare with,' she paused delicately, 'other women you've had?'

'It's different,' he said slowly, seriously considering it.

'Better or worse?'

'I never really thought about it. With you, it's all new,' he sounded as though he were talking to himself. 'It's a little like dying, and a little like being born again. You make me feel—' he searched for the word, then stopped, repeating consideringly, 'You make me *feel*.'

Alicia smiled in the darkness, satisfied, and kissed his throat.

They returned from Hawaii suntanned and wind-blown. The flowers in Alicia's hair shivered and grew limp in the first blast of English winter. But nothing could chill Alicia's pleasure at not having to check in with Aunt Elizabeth.

They drove straight to the house. It stood tall and stately in the twilight, several windows alight with welcome. Alicia felt a surge of sudden gladness, her tiredness dropping away. Home. The word had never meant anything before.

After carrying their luggage into the house, and answering some of the daily's, Mrs Larke's, questions before she left, they went through the house. Everything was ready and waiting for them: the kitchen stocked with food, their belongings unpacked and neatly put away, the last of the new furniture delivered. the dining room table was stacked with a mountain of wedding gifts.

They walked outside to the stables and Alicia introduced Dev to his wedding present. She watched his quick pleasure as he examined the tall grey gelding. She realised she was smiling foolishly and turned away, leaving Dev stroking the grey's bony face.

Something about England, perhaps it was the weather, made her feel more inhibited and self-aware than she had for weeks. Dev was quieter, too, more thoughtful. She hoped it was jet lag and not that he didn't like the house. As far as Alicia was concerned life couldn't possibly get better: a lovely house, freedom to do as she liked, and best of all, Dev.

Back in the house, Dev seemed to shake off his moodiness. They went into the kitchen and Alicia uncorked a bottle of champagne while Dev hunted through the refrigerator for something to eat. He settled on omelettes, giving Alicia over the shoulder instructions. She leaned against the counter, sipping her champagne and listening obediently. Her eyes flicked to his brown, chiselled profile; traced the springy wave of his hair.

'It's all in the wrist,' Dev was saying, cracking open an egg in one neat movement. His eyes met hers, green and direct. Alicia's heart flipped over. Their eyes held for a moment, then each looked away, and Alicia felt her heart beat a little faster.

When the omelettes were cooked, they carried their plates and the champagne bottle into the dining-room, to eat while they unwrapped the wedding gifts. There were a great many presents Alicia doubted they would find much use for: silver tea-sets, crystal goblets and decanters, hand-stitched linens, lace cloths and dusters, solid gold bud vases. Dev's crowd gave designer sheets, plants, a clock in a great chunk of tree trunk, paintings and ceramics.

Finished with the unwrapping, Dev contrasted the divided piles of who had sent what, and looked wry. Alicia wanted to say something to the effect that she didn't expect, or want, to live in the style of Jacqueline and Victor. She didn't see much use for lace dusters—she showed a tendency for spilling drinks on them. She didn't want to worry about tracking stable debris on plush carpets, or breaking crystalware. If Dev wanted to put the tiger-striped black and mauve sheets on their bed, she was agreeable. If he wanted to hang that tree clock in the drawing room, he was welcome. Anything that made Dev happy, made Alicia happy.

She hoped he understood that. She hoped that now that they were home, and would soon settle into a married routine, he would not grow bored and restless. That he would not resent his lost freedom or become impatient with her family and background. They were so very different, but surely if they loved each other . . . ?

She was almost shaking with nerves by the time they went upstairs. What if it was different now? What if he didn't still want her? She brushed her hair slowly, watching Dev prowl around their room in the mirror's reflection. He reminded her of a cat, exploring new territory. He opened and shut the bureau drawers, examined the closet contents. He looked so lean and virile in the brown pyjama bottoms and nothing else. Her fingers tightened on the brush handle. She was nearly wearing through her scalp. She was terrified of going to bed, in case he didn't want her.

She watched his image cross to the bed and draw back the covers. 'Aren't you coming to bed?' he asked abruptly, facing her in the mirror.

Alicia's spirits lifted heavenwards. She dropped the brush with a clatter on the tray, and stood up, crossing to the bed. Dev watched her from between the sheets as she slid off her robe and snapped out the light on the bedside table. She crawled into bed, and lay demurely beside him.

Almost roughly, he reached out and pulled her towards him. Alicia wound her arms around him, her lips eagerly parting. His mouth pressed hers, the tip of his tongue lightly brushing her upper lip. Alicia's heart began to race, and she pressed more closely against him, feeling through her gown's thin material, his rough chest against her breast's softness. Dev's fingers moved ripplingly down her, taking the gown's hemline and raising it up, to leave her bare and warm against him. His mouth moving more and more urgently over hers.

Alicia responded, to his need and the need within her. Delighted sensation swept all doubts and fears away. She was home, safe.

CHAPTER SIX

THE word 'marriage' had never been synonymous with 'fun' in Alicia's mind. But it was fun, she discovered. At least, it was with the right person. She resumed her studies, signed up for fencing lessons and generally did anything she chose, with Dev's approval. Very little perturbed Dev. He didn't care if she came in grubby from the stables, or made them late, or lost things, or broke things, or forgot to give him his messages, or ate ice cream for breakfast—or skipped it all together. He didn't seem to notice all her little faults that had Aunt Elizabeth and Jacqueline climbing the walls.

They had one argument only in all the first weeks following their return home. Alicia did a short interview for an art magazine series on wives of modern artists. It was a silly little bit on how Alicia coped with her husband's greatness, and what Dev was actually like underneath The Artist.

When Dev found out, he was clearly annoyed. 'I should have told you before,' he said crisply. 'I forgot that it might come up. I never give personal interviews.'

Alicia quailed before his flat displeasure. 'Oh, I'm sorry,' she exclaimed repentantly. 'But it was so harmless I didn't think it mattered.'

'It matters to me. I like my private life kept private.'

'It was just questions like what you prefer for breakfast,' Alicia offered.

'It's nobody's business what I prefer for break-fast,' Dev stated. 'Don't defend yourself, Alicia; admit that you made a mistake and take care not to repeat it.'

He didn't say it coldly or rudely, but with such sternness that Alicia felt she were facing her old school headmistress. It was a new perspective on Dev. He made her feel foolish, and she resented his attitude. She had been rather proud of coming out publically as Mrs Devereaux Rafferty. Suddenly she saw how his faults could affect her: he was arrogant and self-absorbed—not through vanity, but through a solitary lifetime's habit of referring only to himself, and what he wanted. But the thought of his not loving her filled her with such dread that she pushed aside her resentment.

'I really am sorry, Dev,' she faltered.

He shrugged it aside, flickering her cheek with a casual finger. 'Never mind,' he told her.

She was rather subdued, not expecting it to end there, but to her grateful relief, he never mentioned the matter again. He didn't try to punish her in any of the subtle ways Aunt Elizabeth would have. There was no coolness in his manner: no withdrawal. He wasn't being magnanimous, she realised later, he had honestly dismissed the incident. It was things like that made her love him.

On the whole, Alicia felt their marriage was a success. The Raffertys got along very well: no quarrels, no frustrations, no disappointments. And it would get better, she knew, as she grew to understand Dev more completely. She was learning all the time. He was still difficult about money matters, although he didn't object to anything spent on Alicia or the house. So much for Aunt Elizabeth and her crowd's fears of fortune-hunting.

In April, Alicia took her exams, passing with flying colours. Dev finished her second portrait and they hung it over the fireplace in the drawing room. He began preparing for another exhibition at Maxwell's. Life was a comfortable routine, and the months passed.

Eventually, Alicia knew, they were bound to run into Magda Morrison. Dev had already seen her a few times at people's houses. It was inevitable, as she and Dev belonged to the same social and artistic circles. Each party they went to, each exhibition, Alicia warned herself that this might be the time. But it never was and she began to relax, thinking Magda was perhaps avoiding them.

They had been married about four months when they did come face to face with her. It was at a party, very like the first party they met at. Dev was off talking to someone or getting drinks, Alicia turned and there was Magda looking coolly up into her face. Alicia stiffened, then made herself relax and make some polite greeting.

'I thought it was you,' Magda remarked, her lovely violet eyes assessing Alicia frankly. 'You've changed. Marriage suits you.' Magda watched her, small and intense, like a cat.

'Yes, it does,' Alicia responded, not trusting this sudden cordiality.

'It suits Dev, as well,' Magda said with a rather contemptuous smile. 'Or at least the money does.'

'Dev didn't marry me for my money,' Alicia said coldly.

Magda continued to smile, amused and scornful.

'He didn't!' Alicia snapped.

'He could hardly have been in love with both of us,' Magda pointed out.

'He wasn't in love with you. It was over. He threw you out.'

'Yes, he did. But not because he didn't love me. He loved me in his own way—it just wasn't enough. He loved your money more.'

'I'm not going to listen to this,' Alicia started to walk away and Magda caught her arm with surprising strength.

'Believe it or not, I'm telling you for *your* sake.'

'I'll bet!'

'Don't be stupid. I like things fine as they are.' she smiled a sly little smile, eyes wide and inquiring.

'What do you mean?' Alicia asked tightly. 'Are you trying to say Dev is seeing you still?'

'Well, we're *bound* to run into each other,' Magda purred. 'I'm sure he's told you that. He is out a lot, isn't he? Visiting friends and such?'

Alicia jerked her wrist away, not caring who saw. 'It won't work,' she told the other woman icily. 'You're trying to get back at us because Dev threw you out.'

'Why do you suppose Dev "threw" me out, as you so quaintly put it?' Magda demanded. 'We fought like cat and dog always. Why throw me out *then*? After living together for months? We suited each other. We were used to each other. Yet when little Miss Moneybags wanders in, all blushing adoration, he shows me the door. Suspiciously good timing, I'd say, wouldn't you?' She looked malicious.

'He threw you out because you tore up the portrait.'

Magda smiled slowly. 'That would seem to be the only possible explanation. Except—' she paused delicately, '—I tore the painting up *after* he told me he was going to marry you.'

It seemed hours later when Magda added cordially, 'Ask him, he's a poor liar.'

'You're a good one,' Alicia returned with quiet contempt.

The slightest tinge of red touched Magda's dramatically pale features. She shrugged. 'Believe what you choose.' She looked past Alicia and said pleasantly, 'See you around.'

Alicia glanced behind as Dev joined her, handing her a drink.

'What did she want?' he asked softly.

'To congratulate us,' Alicia was proud of how unruffled she sounded, 'in her own way.' She couldn't meet his eyes.

'Yeah. Do you want to go?' He sounded edgy.

She did, but she asked as though mildly surprised, 'So soon?'

'If you don't mind?'

'I don't mind.' Was he afraid of what Magda might say to her? She followed him out through the swarm of people, smiling and nodding replies to questions and comments she didn't hear. She felt very calm, very reasonable. All she needed was to be alone so she could think this out. She was glad that Dev was uncommunicative on the drive home. She didn't want to talk to him now, so she curled up in the front seat, pretending to sleep. He drove silently and she watched him from her corner. He looked as he always did, but she was seeing him in a new light.

When they were in the house, turning on the lamps, she felt his gaze on her. She tried to act naturally, but she still couldn't quite look at him. She went upstairs ahead, washed and undressed. Looking at the neatly made bed, she felt sick. She sat down at the dressing-table and stared at herself in the mirror. Her face looked perfectly normal. Picking up her hair brush, she began brushing her hair for the sake of something to do.

Dev came up a little later and sat down on the edge of the bed, watching her.

'Did she say something to upset you?' he queried.

'No.' Her tone held just the right amount of bewilderment. Life with Aunt Elizabeth had perfected her talent for deception. 'Why do you ask?'

'You're very quiet.' Was she generally a blabbermouth?

'I'm very tired.' She looked up then, meeting his eyes coolly in the mirror. He studied her for a long moment then got up and began undressing, his back to her. Alicia put down the brush, rose and went to the bed. She slid in, snapped off her light and lay down. A few moments later Dev shut off his light and got in beside her. He slipped his arm around her and she said politely,

'I'm awfully tired.'

Instantly he withdrew his arm. 'Of course.' He sounded equally polite, equally cool. Maybe it was a relief to him. He gave up easily enough.

Alicia lay on her side, her back to him, thinking, *I should ask him. I should ask him now. I'm not being fair.* She stared into the darkness, at the outlines of familiar objects now concealed by the gloom.

I know it's not true. I know he loves me, I can tell. All I have to do is ask him. I know her, she would have said anything to hurt us. She lay silent while he shifted restlessly. *It's stupid to lie here hurting both of us. What am I afraid of?*

She remained still, watching the minutes flip by on the red face of the digital clock. An hour passed, sixty clicks of the clock.

He was still awake. She could tell by his breathing and restive movements. She could ask him right now and get this settled once and for all. But she lay motionless, thinking, and another hour ticked by.

'Are you awake?' Dev asked softly.

She stayed still, breathing gently, her eyes staring straight ahead. She heard him sigh, and a moment later the bed creaked under him as he sat up. He rose, padding quietly across the floor and out into the hall. Alicia rolled over. His side of the bed was still warm.

I have to know, she realised fiercely. *I can't go on not knowing.* But if she asked him and he lied? Or if she asked him and he *admitted* it? She couldn't bear it. She would die. It *wasn't* true. But if it was? She had to know. But not from him. Besides, if it wasn't true he would be furious at her doubt. Her lack of faith would be worse than insulting; it would be unforgivable. Bad enough that other people thought like that. She remembered Aunt Elizabeth and Jacqueline and Victor: their knowing faces. She felt physically ill. She wanted to cry, but he might be back any minute.

She wondered what he was doing? It was the first night since their marriage that insomnia had plagued him. Guilty conscience?

It was another two hours before Alicia slept. Dawn smouldered through the windows, a smoky pink. When she finally drifted off, Dev still hadn't returned . . .

He was sleeping when she rose the next morning. Alicia dressed quietly, slipping into a red cotton blouse he had picked for her, pulling on a cream-coloured, layered skirt. She watched him as she dressed, like a thief riffling through drawers. He slept in exhausted abandon, the chestnut hair tumbled, the penetrating eyes shielded by long coppery lashes. Even in sleep his mouth had a closed look, like he was holding something back. It was not a vulnerable, defenceless face in sleep or any time else. It was too chiselled, too perfect, like a Renaissance marble— one of those sly angels; he looked beautiful and secretive.

She left him sleeping and drove into town. Last night Alicia had made a decision, and her few hours' sleep had not changed it. But this had to be done correctly. No one, least of all Dev, must ever know. There must be no hint of scandal. She would have to arrange it all herself, because she couldn't go to Mr Ellis; word must never get back to her family. Maybe underneath it, she was more of a Carrington than she knew.

Alicia parked at the first phone-box she came to, and thumbed through the directory till she found what she needed. She took down the listing and drove to the address given. Stephens & Son was small and dingy. A dreary little office for dreary people. She parked and went in. Within thirty minutes she had hired herself a private investigator.

She didn't require half of the services they offered. No intercepted mail, no phone taps, no photographs. She simply wanted a weekly report on where he went and who he saw. She understood from their manner that this was a routine request. They managed to make her feel sordid and desperate; they really were a disreputable little operation, and she couldn't help feeling guilty about turning Dev over to them. It smacked of betrayal. But Dev would never know about it—if he were innocent.

Alicia drove home. Mrs Larke informed her that Mr Rafferty was in his studio.

'Then I won't disturb him,' Alicia said briskly. Mrs Larke was surprised. The Raffertys were the closest thing to inseparable she anticipated seeing in her lifetime. 'Disturb' each other was practically all they did.

Alicia went upstairs and changed into jeans and a T-shirt. All was quiet down the hall in the studio. She went down to the kitchen, grabbed an apple and walked out to the stable. If Dev were looking out his window, he would see her and think it odd she hadn't come up to say hi. Already she missed him.

She couldn't keep avoiding Dev for ever. Sooner or later—and probably within the next hour—she was going to be face to face with him. She was going to have to act normally or he would want to know why. She wondered how long it would be before she knew. Knew what? If he was still seeing Magda, then she knew Magda was telling the truth all the way. But if he wasn't seeing Magda it didn't prove that he *hadn't* married Alicia for her money. One thing at a time. She would take the first problem and deal with that. Her major concern was how to deal with Dev interim.

It was nearly teatime when she returned to the house. Mr Rafferty, Mrs Larke told her, was still in his studio. The light was too poor for painting; Alicia wondered exactly what he was doing up there? She told Mrs Larke to take Dev's tea-tray up and went into the den, ignoring Mrs Larke's amazement. *The honeymoon is over*, she thought grimly, reading the other woman's face.

Wondering how to spend her time, Alicia eventually dug up a half-read mystery novel and settled down determinedly.

She had made no noticeable progress in the book when Dev came down for dinner. Her heart automatically leaped up as he strolled into the room, looking lean and attractive in jeans and an old cotton khaki shirt rolled up to his elbows.

He dropped a quick kiss on the top of Alicia's bent head and stretched out on the couch across from her. The slanted eyes watched her reluctantly lay the book aside.

'Had a good day?' he asked. 'I didn't hear you go out this morning.'

'I've had better. How was yours?' she replied with proper wifely interest.

He shrugged lazily, his eyes never leaving her face. She gazed back, ignoring the mute inquiry she read.

'What are you reading?' he queried after a moment.

She held up the lurid cover briefly.

'Mm.' Amusement lightened his eyes. 'Scholarly stuff.'

'Entertaining, anyway.'

He got up in one lithe movement and her nerves jumped. 'Did you want a drink?' he asked over his shoulder, going to the bar.

'No thanks.' She could have used one, but she didn't want him coming that close to her. She watched him unstop the bottle and pour a stiff Scotch.

He wandered back, glass in hand, saying, 'Tomorrow I've got to drive in to Maxwell's. The exhibition starts Monday.'

'That's right.' She had forgotten the exhibition in the day's mental turmoil. The exhibition could come in useful. The idea of trying to avoid Dev for the next two or three weeks seemed more impossible by the minute. Already he was frowning at her evident mental confusion over the event. He opened his mouth, but Mrs Larke poked her head round the door, informing them dinner was ready.

Conversation was desultory during the meal. Alicia picked at her food and noticed Dev did the same. He was drinking more than usual, but she avoided the alcohol. She didn't want to loosen up—she might start saying things she would later regret. She might give in to the lonely little voice inside that told her to forget this mess and take shelter in Dev's warm, comforting arms.

It was a relief to return to the den. She buried herself with manifest enjoyment in her mystery novel, while Dev roamed restlessly around the room. Although apparently absorbed in her reading, she was aware of him with every particle in her body. When he finally flung himself down to watch TV, Alicia felt both deliverance and amusement: delivered, now that he was occupied; amused, knowing how he hated TV. It was odd how one could know so much about another person, and yet not know anything at all.

The evening dragged. At eleven o'clock he switched off the TV set, saying brusquely, 'Will you be up soon?'

'Just as soon as I finish this,' she answered, keeping her face in the book.

She spent the next three hours staring blankly from the ceiling to the unturned page. When she felt enough time had lapsed, she crept quietly upstairs, undressed in the dark, and slipped between the sheets, staying well to her side of the bed. She thought he was asleep. In any case, he lay quietly beside her, not speaking or moving. Emotionally exhausted, Alicia fell rapidly into sleep.

The next morning he was gone when she woke, she was sleeping when he returned that evening. It initiated their pattern for the next week. The exhibition made it easier to avoid each other. She was not sure whether Dev were deliberately avoiding her, or whether it was just working out that way, but she was glad of the respite. She realised that Dev was aware of something being wrong, but since he didn't broach the matter, she didn't worry. She stayed busy with letters, books, lessons, riding and anything else she could think of. She missed Dev all the time. After his first attempts to talk to her and touch her, he withdrew completely. His manner matched Alicia's own for cool cordiality. It was hard to go on living like that, knowing it was her fault, knowing that it might be unnecessary, but Carrington pride held her to her course. Besides, she was a little miffed that he cared so little about her withdrawal, that he just accepted it.

At the end of the first week Alicia received her initial report from Stephens & Son. She read it with shaking hands. Until then she had not considered what she would actually do if Dev was seeing Magda. As she scanned the sheets she was aware of profound gratitude that she did not—yet—have to decide.

She felt terrible reading over the careful little diary of Dev's life. An entire week, entirely innocent. She remembered promising him he would have his freedom in their marriage; that she believed married people should not try to own each other. She remembered him saying that he liked his private life kept private. She was acting like the worst kind of paranoid; like the kind of women she despised. *But it's his fault*, she thought childishly, and knew that for the pathetic excuse it was.

She tore the report up in tiny pieces and flushed them down the toilet. She nearly called up Stephens & Son to dismiss them, but caught herself. One more week, maybe two, and she would know for sure. She would never doubt him again. It was worth it, surely?

When Dev returned home that afternoon she was warmer than she had been in days: chatty and affectionate. He responded politely, which chilled her enthusiasm a little. It was her own fault if he didn't respond delightedly when she chose to be friendly again; comprehension didn't make her feel any better. She had a bit to make up for. It was going to be hard to start up cordial relations with no explanation. But with time she was certain everything could go back to normal. Already she was more than half-convinced of his innocence. Next week's report was just a technicality. Six months from now she would be laughing about this—to herself.

Wednesday of the second week, was Mrs Larke's day off. Alicia was cooking dinner, or considering it, when she heard the front door slam with a violence reverberating all the way to the kitchen. She stood, eyes wide with sudden foreboding, surrounded by open cook books and bowls. Dev appeared in the kitchen doorway. She needed no second look at his white, furious face to know the worst had somehow happened. She swallowed nervously as his eyes, so dark they looked black, raked her up and down contemptuously.

'You won't be getting your weekly report,' he bit

out before she could speak. 'Maybe I can fill you in on the details of—' he shoved a kitchen table chair aside with barely restraining rage, coming towards Alicia, 'where I go, who I see and what I do!'

She had never even heard him raise his voice before, and her knees weakened with fear, her mouth went desert dry. He was literally shaking with fury. He stood a foot away, and though Alicia was nearly as tall as he, he seemed to tower menacingly over her.

'How did you find out?' Her voice sounded high and young.

'I *knocked* it out of my *tail*,' he grated, holding his fist up as though he wanted to do the same to her. She winced, seeing the knuckles puffy, grazed, the blood drying.

'Did you think I wouldn't *notice* someone tailing me everywhere I went? How stupid do you think I am?'

She said unsteadily, 'I'm sorry—' She was, desperately. Not merely because of his frightening anger, but because she saw her actions through his eyes and knew how unforgivably she had acted.

'*Sorry?*' He jerked out. 'Oh! Well! What the hell! All is forgiven! Would you like to read my mail, maybe?' He stared at her with utter scorn, saying bitterly, 'How could you *do* such a thing? What did you imagine you'd find?'

'I thought you were still Magda's lover,' she told him honestly.

His anger seemed to drain away, giving ground to disbelief. '*Magda?* That's what this is all about? That's what these *weeks* of cold shoulder have been about?' He stared at her and said stingingly, 'How could you think that of me?'

'She said so. She said you only married me for my

money. She said you were still lovers. I had to know if it was true.'

'Why didn't you *ask*?'

She couldn't answer. His eyes took in her expression and he turned to leave. Alicia caught his arm, feeling the taut muscles beneath his shirt. 'Dev, I know you're not her lover,' she said distraughtly. 'Just tell me you married me because you loved me.'

He gave her a long, immobile look. She read it in his eyes. She remembered Magda saying he was unable to lie. She felt almost nauseous with shock.

'I love you,' Dev said flatly. 'You know I do.'

She blinked, trying to focus on his face. 'Did you love me when you married me?' she demanded, her nails biting into his arm. At his silence she said tensely, '*Did you?*' He didn't answer and she flung away from him, sick and bitter.

'*Yes*, I loved you!' he said savagely. 'How could I help it? You were such an engaging child. Of course I loved you! But I wasn't *in* love with you!'

'I see,' she said in dead tones, her back to him.

'No, you don't,' he said angrily. 'You don't see it at all. What does it matter now how I felt then? Since Hawaii I've known I loved you. I *am* in love with you.'

'Are you? Or are you in love with this life-style?' she shot over her shoulder.

'If it had just been the money I wouldn't have done it,' he said.

'Wouldn't you have?' she turned to him, her face white, her eyes bright with unshed tears. 'Tell me this, if I *hadn't* had the money, if I had been an engaging child *without* a fortune to sweeten the deal, would you *still* have married me?'

He faced her, not speaking, his eyes burning with emotion.

'No,' Alicia answered drily, 'you wouldn't have.'

'It's not that simple,' he retorted, vehemently. 'I *didn't* intend to marry you; I tried then to explain how I felt about you. You wouldn't listen. The more you talked, the harder it was. You were so eager and intense and starved of affection.'

'And rich,' put in Alicia cynically.

'I wasn't *thinking* about the money—not then. I was sorry for you, if you want to know. I didn't know how to explain that I didn't feel what you seemed to—my God, I wasn't sure what *you* felt underneath all the hero-worship! Then, you were so insistent, so persuasive—I admit it! I thought, why not? You wanted it so desperately. I knew for damn sure I would be kinder to you than your family. It seemed a fair exchange. You were so hungry for attention and affection, I knew it would be only a matter of time before you were involved with someone—anyone— else. At least I cared about you . . .'

She hated him. She hated him for reading her so well, for using her needs, for *pitying* her. She hated him nearly as much as she hated the lonely, naïve, *pathetic* girl she had been. She looked at him and she hated him. She was sick and trembling with it. She could hardly breathe or speak; it rose, choking her.

She heard him saying, 'It wasn't like I *planned* it out ahead of time. It wasn't calculated. It was spontaneous. My God, I *was* in love with you not a month later. Do I have to spend the rest of my life paying for that impulse?'

Alicia said in an ice-cold voice, 'Why did you break off with Magda?'

'It was over. It had been for a long time. The portrait was the last straw.'

She smiled with malignant triumph. 'That's interesting. Magda says she ruined the portrait *after* you told her to go. Is that true?'

His eyes flickered. 'That's true,' he said without expression.

'Really? *And* she says she destroyed the portrait because you told her—weeks before *I* ever thought of the idea—that you were going to marry me.' She watched him, eyes glittering, absorbing his shock.

'I said it to her. I wasn't serious,' he protested.

'Are you sure it wasn't in the back of your mind all along? After all, you couldn't help but see how I idolised you, and how "affection starved" I was. Are you *sure* you didn't *subconsciously* get Magda out of the way, so that when I proposed to you, you'd be in a position to accept?'

Dev said with helpless frustration, 'I don't know! Do you think I haven't wondered? Do you think I don't feel guilty—loving you?'

'I'm sure it's been a terrible ordeal,' Alicia said with contempt. 'But your ordeal is through. I want you to go.'

'Alicia, will you give me a chance?' he exclaimed, catching her wrist.

'I've given you enough,' she said. At the cutting scorn in her voice and face, he dropped his hold on her. 'Maybe I should be grateful. It could have been worse. You were rather *kind*, and you certainly taught me a lot. But I'm not that pathetic, clinging, little fool any longer and I don't need your *services*. I think I've paid an awfully high price for them as it is.'

His face was expressionless, eyes narrowed. He was very pale. 'Listen to me—' he said urgently.

'I never want to hear or see you again,' she ground out fiercely.

He stepped towards her, and she screamed hysterically:

'Get out of my house!'

He stopped, turned on his heel and walked, without a word, from the room. A second later she heard the front door slam.

'*Damn* you!' she cried and grabbed one of the bowls on the counter beside her, smashing it on the floor.

CHAPTER SEVEN

ALICIA woke to hot sunlight streaming through the
bedroom windows. She lay for a minute, blinking
tiredly, wondering at the shadow of depression she
felt pass over her. What was wrong? Then she remembered: Dev was gone. Nearly three weeks had
passed since the terrible fight in the kitchen.

Two days after the fight, he had returned, while
she was down at the paddock, and packed up most of
his art things, along with some clothes and basic
necessities. She wondered if he had some belated
pride about not taking anything she had paid for. A
third of the things he had left had been his own when
they married, and she had news for him if he imagined he could pay her back in socks and after-
shave. He hadn't come down to the stables, and
Alicia had not known he had been home till after he
had gone. He had not left any message for her, but
that was a message in itself, she supposed.

Maybe the days weren't as long and empty for
Dev. Who knew what he might be filling his life with?
She wondered where he was living? With whom?
Of course, it was different for Dev. For him it was
just a matter of readjusting to a life-style he hadn't
had to grow unaccustomed to. For her, it was trying to rebuild a life on the emotional ruins of the
past.

She admitted painfully that there was not an
aspect of her life he had not influenced: from hair,
make-up and clothes, right down to how she felt

about herself. She was an entirely different woman today because of Dev Rafferty.

She had learned to see herself as a worthwhile person, an attractive woman. She had grown confident and sure under his indulgent eye. And, thanks to Dev, she knew now what it was like to have that confidence, that security, jerked out from under. She had made the full circle from a plain, insecure, lonely girl to an attractive, insecure, lonely woman.

It had taken her three weeks to realise that she did have a life without Dev. She had not recognised before how closely intertwined her life was with his. How much she depended on his support and reassurance. For three days after he had gone, she had burst into tears at the thought of him. She still cried every night, alone in her big, cold bed. She dreamed about him, she dreamed their fight over and over. She couldn't eat, she didn't want to see anyone or go anywhere or do anything.

But that had to stop. She had to forget Dev. She had to build a new life on the salvageable ruins of the old. To do that, she needed a purpose. She needed to keep busy. She needed a job. After she had married Dev she had postponed her previous intentions of getting a job. There had seemed plenty of time and she had wanted to spend as much of it as possible with her husband. But the more she thought about it, the better she liked the idea. She had her hard-won degree, she had connections. There were a number of places she could work. For the first time in three weeks, she felt a lick of enthusiasm.

Her job hunt began and ended with Mr Mawell.

'But my dear Mrs Rafferty,' Mr Maxwell exclaimed, when she called to ask for referrals, '*I* could use you!'

'You?' Alicia's surprise was not all pleasant. Dev was closely connected with Maxwell's.

'But of course!' Mr Maxwell sounded astonished at her doubt. 'With your credentials—'

Alicia read between the lines. Beyond her education, she had dozens of wealthy friends, and the prestige attached to being the wife of one of the day's foremost artists. She considered bringing up her separation from Dev, but there was no point. Mr Maxwell knew. He hadn't tried contacting her to reach Dev, indicating he knew where Dev was. That was more than Alicia knew. If Mr Maxwell wanted the soon-to-be ex-Mrs Rafferty, who was she to argue? She needed a job.

'Why don't you drop in and we'll chat about it?' Mr Maxwell was saying persuasively, as though anticipating her reluctance.

'Well—' Alicia hesitated, then gave up. She couldn't hide from what had happened. 'All right,' she agreed.

She agreed again after Mr Maxwell talked to her about the job when she went to the Gallery. He was so persuasive, so tactful about her separation. Besides, she liked the Gallery; it was familiar and secure.

She liked the job, too. It wasn't very difficult, just looking decorative and chatting knowledgeably about art to connoisseurs. Many of Maxwell's clients were friends of her family, buying merely because it was Alicia showing them around. Happily, she did not see many of Dev's friends. This was the buying, not the creative end of the art world. Few of Dev's friends could afford what their own paintings would be worth one day.

In the days that passed she saw nothing of Dev. She was relieved but curious. She would have asked Mr Maxwell about him, but pride forbade it. She didn't know what she would do if she did run into him.

She wondered what he was living on. He hadn't touched their bank account, although some of the money in it was his from his paintings. He must be living on commissions, practically hand to mouth. She didn't feel guilty or impressed—Dev was more than capable of looking out for himself. Maybe he had found a new patron.

In September Aunt Elizabeth and Jacqueline returned from their cruise, and Alicia went to see each of them, to tell the truth. It was a pride-grinding experience, as she had known it would be. She remembered her defiant insistence on marrying Dev; she hated him all over again for proving them right.

'You must divorce him immediately,' Aunt Elizabeth stated, when Alicia had told her the bare bones. She looked tanned and fit from her vacation; her eyes lit up at Alicia's painful recital.

'What about the scandal?' Alicia asked.

'People will realise the truth: you were young and naïve. This unscrupulous man took advantage of you.'

'I'll look like a fool,' she protested.

'You have been a fool,' Aunt Elizabeth said coldly.

She had, and she hadn't expected any sympathy from Aunt Elizabeth, but she resented the assumption that she would meekly advertise the fact to the world. She equally resented Aunt Elizabeth's supposition that she was incapable of handling her own

affairs. She had managed to get along an entire
month now without Dev or Aunt Elizabeth.

'You must have him found,' Aunt Elizabeth continued, unaware of the brewing rebellion. 'You must
hire someone reliable.'

'No!' Alicia stood up. 'I'm not having Dev treated
like a criminal.' Though things had turned out as
they had, she still regretted having had him spied on.
That had been unforgivable of *her*.

Aunt Elizabeth's pale blue eyes narrowed. 'What
do you mean, Alicia?'

'I can find Dev without having him hunted down.'

'Good God!' her aunt said sharply. 'Aren't you
dramatising slightly? I'm not suggesting we call out
the hounds. But need I remind you that the less you
have to do with this man, the better? I sincerely hope
you aren't dreaming of some *reconciliation*?'

'Of course not!' Alicia paced before the cold fireplace with nervous energy. 'I want *nothing* to do with
him. As soon as I feel ready, I'm going to sue for
divorce.'

Later, Alicia thought about Aunt Elizabeth's determined plans for her future and was filled with
frustration.

Perhaps she should see Dev? It was childish to
drift along not knowing what he had in mind. In a
way, Aunt Elizabeth and Jacqueline were right:
there was no point in delaying. The longer she
waited, the more complicated—and embarrassing—
the matter would be. Soon her separation would be
advertised to the world by her family. People would
wonder at her reluctance, and they might think she
was pathetic enough to still love Dev. She should act
right away.

Mr Maxwell seemed oddly happy to give her

Dev's address. Perhaps he was hoping for a reconciliation—he'd be the only one. He wished her luck
and Alicia thanked him. She wasn't in any hurry to
face Dev, so she waited till the weekend, driving into
town Saturday morning.

He was living not far from his original home. The
neighbourhood was poorer, the traffic worse. Alicia
parked her car an intersection away and walked the
short distance to the flat. It was ugly and modern, a
depressing place, and she couldn't imagine Dev
living there.

She went inside and rang the bell at his door, but
there was no answer. She could hardly swallow her
disappointment. It had been difficult steeling herself
to come, and finding him out was an unexpected
blow.

Reluctantly she went back downstairs and stood
for a while on the pavement, thinking. Two teenage
boys whizzed by on a motorbike, making catcalls.
Alicia gave up and recrossed the street.

She waited on the corner for the light to change,
and glancing back, saw a tall, familiar figure going
into the building carrying a paper sack: Dev. Her
heart jumped with instant recognition. She saw
someone greet him at the entrance, talking earnestly.
Dev looked back outside and his companion pointed
out Alicia, dithering nervously on the corner. Dev
handed his bag to the other with a word of thanks,
and came down the steps, graceful and unhurried.
He started across the street.

Alicia stood, hands thrust in her pockets, chin up,
watching him dodge his way. He looked cool, almost
bored, and she felt her muscles tighten as she waited.
He reached her, saying sardonically, 'If it isn't
Nancy Drew.'

'I'm not spying on you,' Alicia snapped. He had changed very little. He was still devastatingly attractive in a grey lambswool sweater and jeans. His hair looked longer, more unruly, and there was a fine, taut look to his face, as though he were perpetually grim. He looked grim enough now. No amusement in the green, slanted eyes; no charming smile. No warmth, no friendliness, not even surprise. But then, Alicia supposed she didn't look particularly cordial either, scowling aggressively at him.

He said, in answer to her, 'You just happened to be in the neighbourhood?'

'I came to see you. I wanted to talk to you.'

'About what?' He was like stone: hard, immovable. He stared at her and Alicia stared back, just as cold and steady.

'I have a proposition.' That came out impulsively. She was surprised to hear the words.

'What?'

'Do we have to talk *here*?' she looked around at the crowded street and pavement.

'I'm busy. I don't have a lot of time to waste. Say it.' She couldn't believe Dev—amused, indulgent, patient Dev—could be talking to her like this.

She said stiffly, 'I want you to come back—on my terms.'

There was a long moment of silence while he studied her with narrowed eyes.

'What are your—terms?' he asked finally.

'It would be a marriage in name only. You get the money—which is all that matters to you, isn't it? I get to face the world with a loving, devoted husband by my side—in public, which is all I really care about.' Her cynicism caused his eyes to flicker.

Dev said slowly, 'You're all Carrington after all,

aren't you? All that matters is the appearance of things?'

'Maybe. What do you care? You get what you want. All I demand is that you pretend—you found it easy enough before—to be devoted. We can have a contract drawn up. You'll have your freedom, within limits, and all the money you could possibly need.' She had toyed with the idea before, not really acknowledging its possibilities. Now that it was in words, she realised what she had wanted all along.

He said with disgust, 'Since when do you care what people like your Aunt Elizabeth think? You can't buy loyalty or respect. You used to know that. You can't buy people. I'm not your possession. I'm not for sale.'

'Since when?' she questioned, sarcastically.

He went white, his expression frightening. Alicia stepped back as Dev said with deadly intensity, 'You couldn't touch the price. There isn't money enough in the world to pay me to touch you with a stick.'

Then he left her standing still with shock at the hate she had seen in his eyes, heard in his voice. She frozenly watched him weaving his way with reckless disregard across the street.

People walking past stared at her silent, rigid figure with brief curiosity. She watched Dev, not really even thinking. He was nearly to the kerb.

The truck seemed to appear out of nowhere. It was like a dream. Dev simply didn't see it bearing down on him. There was a sudden, last-minute squeal of breaks, and a high, desperate scream—her own, Alicia realised later. She heard the sickening thud, and then she was running, blind, uncaring. There were shouts, honking, and slamming breaks behind her; she didn't know. She wasn't aware of anything but his tumbled body: motionless, still . . .

It seemed to Alicia that she had spent her entire life waiting in the hospital. Nothing else was real, but sitting, drinking endless cups of black coffee, hearing the same worn phrase: 'Sorry, no change.'

It felt like months, years, but it had only been a week. The longest week of her life. *Just let him wake up*, she prayed. *I don't care if he hates me. I don't care if I never get to see him again. Just let him be all right.* She lived every second of the week in exhausted terror. She was too desperate to be numb. She couldn't sleep or eat. She could only wait. Her life seemed to revolve around one urgent question: 'How is he?'

He was not good. He was critically injured, comatose, his skull fractured. Dr Andrews explained everything very carefully to Alicia. But really, there was little to explain. He would either wake up or he wouldn't. She knew, though no one said so, that the longer he stayed in the coma, the less likely he would be to wake up.

They had operated; successfully, they told her, which meant nothing, really. They let her see him through an observation window. His head had been shaved, and was wrapped in white swathing. He lay motionless in the crisp, white bed. There were tubes and bottles everywhere. The only sign that he was still alive was the rhythmic jump of green on the monitor beside his bed. She watched it blip, praying.

The hospital staff were very kind. Dr Andrews was Alicia's own doctor. She had known him since her teens. She had had a riding accident and Aunt Elizabeth's doctor was unavailable. Dr Andrews had stepped in, and Alicia had kept him as her physician despite her aunt's displeasure. It was one of the first battles she had won.

She trusted Dr Andrews. He kept her informed, as much as possible, on what was happening. She knew he had contacted Dr Wallace Wales, the American neuro-surgeon, and had him flown to the hospital. Dr Wales was the best in his field, and Dr Wales said there was no reason to despair. They gave Alicia a small, private room where she could wait and sleep. They tried to persuade her to eat, but otherwise they mostly left her alone, to deal with it as well as she could. That was what she wanted: to be alone, so that she didn't have to pretend she was brave, or optimistic, or anything but desperate.

A week to the day of Devereaux's accident, Dr Wales operated a second time. 'It's not unusual with head injuries,' Dr Andrews reassured her. 'It's not unusual that he should be unconscious this long.' Nobody was giving up hope. A week was nothing. If Dev recovered, he would be months in the hospital, months convalescing.

Day nine, Rafferty woke up. It was just for a moment or two, Dr Andrews informed Alicia, but he had been definitely conscious. It was an excellent sign. To her quick inquiry he reassured her that Dev's eyes were all right. Alicia dropped to the couch too relieved to speak or cry. She slept for the first time in nine days, deep, dreamless sleep; through the day, through the night, through another day. When she woke they had more good news for her.

Dev showed further signs of progress. He was sleeping normally, not unconscious. He understood what was said to him, and though he was too weak to do more than blink, his vital signs were strong.

'Has he—asked for me?' Alicia asked hesitantly the next day. She was prepared, she told herself, to hear that he never wanted to see her again. But her jaw was gritted, her lips pressed tightly together.

Dr Andrews hesitated. There was a problem, he told her carefully. Not unexpected, but a problem all the same.

'What is it?' Alicia demanded steadily.

'Amnesia. Complete memory loss.'

At her blank face, he was quick to reassure her that Dev might regain his memory any day. True, there was *some* chance that he might not regain it at all, but that was rare. Very few people lost their entire memory. It would probably be back within the next week or two.

'What doesn't he remember?' Alicia asked carefully.

Dr Andrews looked rather grave, 'Who he is, for one thing. His complete life is a mystery to him. But, as I say, it's not unusual. Very likely, it will all come back shortly.'

But it didn't. As soon as Dev was strong enough, they explained about Alicia and let her in to see him for a couple of minutes. It was the first time she had seen him actually conscious since the accident. It was also the first time she went in without a surgical mask, as his wife.

It did not seem possible that he would not recognise her. Alicia moved nervously to the side of the bed and looked down. He looked very flat against the pristine white, very still. But his eyes were alive and vividly green in the shockingly bruised pallor of his face. They examined Alicia with intensity, wide and curious. There was no recognition, but there was something else, a lost look that made Alicia put aside her self-consciousness and bend down to kiss his lean, bristly cheek.

'I'm sorry,' he whispered, 'I don't remember.' A person did not forget their nature. There was that old instinctive kindness. He was the one in trouble, but he was sorry for having to hurt her by not knowing her. Alicia straightened, and they looked at each other gravely.

'I remember,' she said softly.

'Yes.' His voice was just a whisper of sound. 'You'll have to tell me.' His fingers stirred a little on the white spread. Alicia slipped her brown, strong hand under his and the long fingers closed tightly. They relaxed as his eyes dropped shut and he slept. Alicia stayed till the nurse came, willing him her strength through the link of their clasped hands.

When she returned to her room she cried for the first time. Cried out her fear and loneliness and relief. Afterwards she felt much better.

Slowly Dev recovered. Dr Wales informed Alicia that, considering the extent of his injuries, he was making excellent progress. The persistent memory-gap was unsettling, but not unusual. Patience was the key. Further X-rays showed nothing to be alarmed about. Mr Rafferty was healing in his own time.

Alicia went daily to the hospital. Mr Maxwell had soothed her qualms about leaving work—she was far more useful to him with Dev, he assured. No one else needed her. She was not responsible to anyone else. Dev was her life. As long as Dev needed her, she would be there, and she would be strong. She was beginning to understand that most people could not relate to that single-minded intensity of feeling. Dev could have. He might not have felt it, but he would have understood it. Maybe that was why she loved him the way she did.

She was careful to keep that love under wraps when she went to the hospital. She was careful about what she did, and careful about what she said. Always she kept in mind that however she felt, she was a stranger to him. He didn't love her, he didn't know her. She tried to imagine how it would be to wake up and know nothing about your past, and have strangers tell you you were their wife or mother or sister. She was very tactful.

When they talked, she limited information to him: his life, his past. She kept herself, and her feelings, completely out, striving to be comfortably impersonal. She didn't know that much about his early life, and she wanted to avoid the possibly uncomfortable topic of their relationship. She had to strain sometimes to avoid it. On those occasions she could sense him registering her efforts, his eyes reading her unspoken evasion.

One day she brought the seascape she had purchased from Maxwell's that first exhibition. She had told Dev earlier that he painted; was a respected figure in the art world. Dr Wales thought it might be a good memory catalyst. But Dev studied the painting, frowning, with no sign of recall. Alicia realised uneasily, after a few moments, that he was tense and upset. She dropped the painting down behind the foot of the bed, saying reassuringly, 'It doesn't matter, Dev. You'll remember soon.'

His eyes flew angrily up to hers. 'What if I don't remember? You don't know how it feels. It's like being lost in another world. Everyone knows me, but I know *nothing*. I wouldn't know my name if you didn't tell me.' His eyes were dark with frustration, his face growing flushed. She went to his side, pressing him back against the pillows.

'Dev, you must lie still,' she soothed, with a nervous glance towards the door.

'Leave me alone!' he said fiercely, and bewilderedly she dropped her hands away. 'You've no understanding,' he bit out. 'You tell me my parents are dead and I have no family. You tell me you're my wife, but I don't know you. I don't feel anything for you. I have nothing, I have no one!'

His breathing grew strained, his face grey.

'You've got to calm down,' Alicia said frightenedly, reaching again to him. 'Dev, I'm going to call the doctor—'

'No.' His hands caught hers. He slumped, drained, against the pillows. 'Please—' He licked his lips and Alicia turned to pour him a glass of water, her hands unsteady. She held the glass to his pale lips, her hand supporting his thickly bandaged head. He drank, then lay exhausted against the pillows. Alicia removed the pillows so that he lay flat, and he looked up, his eyes shadowy. His voice was a whisper.

'Sorry. It's not your fault.' His eyes flickered. He turned his head, watching her. His eyes had a frowning, puzzled look. 'I've *got* to remember.'

'You will.'

His lids drooped and he slept.

After his reaction to the painting, Alicia tried a new tack when she went to visit Dev. Now she told him about herself; initially basic facts, like her age and her schooling and her hobbies and family anecdotes. When he seemed to actually be listening, she told him other things, like how she felt and what she thought. He attended very carefully, his eyes steady on hers. It was as though he were listening for the message beneath the spoken one. See, Alicia was telling him, I'm no stranger. What do you want to know?

She told him briefly about their courtship, and she left a great deal of unpleasantness—like Magda—out. She told him about Hawaii, blushing at what she was expurgating, and for the first time since his accident, he grinned faintly, watching her. She told him about trips they had made, things they had done, as well as plans for what they would do. She was trying to build him a sense of stability, of continuity in their relationship. She was reaching out, to give him a chance to catch an emotional foothold. And each day she could feel him taking a firmer grip, winning back equilibrium.

She told him about their house; encouraging things. She told him how cool and green the surrounding grounds were. How peaceful and quiet; things to hearten someone who had been two months in hospital already. She told him about the horses, and the woods not far away. She could see interest lighten the shadows in his eyes. His indifferent struggle to get well gained purpose, energy. Alicia realised that she had been wrong to be so impersonally friendly. He had enough of that from the hospital staff. She was the only person he knew, the only person he had to turn to in the mental dark. He hadn't needed her proof that he was independent and free; he needed reassurance he wasn't alone.

Nearly three months after the accident, Alicia brought Dev home. She felt rather triumphant, as if she had grabbed off first prize in a tough competition. He was a somewhat battered prize. In a way he looked worse out of bed than he had in. For a recovering patient, he had been in fairly good shape; as walking wounded, he barely qualified. He was very thin, unattractively thin, and so white he looked transparent. There were no signs of his injuries, except that his hair was still short and surprisingly curly. But he was moving on his own power, however slowly.

Mrs Larke met them at the door, saying effusively, 'It's good to have you home, Mr Rafferty!'

Alicia noted with surprise that Mrs Larke actually had unshed tears in her eyes. *She cares about us. We belong here. We really had built a home together.*

'Thank you—' Dev glanced at Alicia '—Mrs Larke.'

'We'll have you strong again in no time,' Mrs Larke told him. She sniffed, saying briskly to Alicia, 'Lunch will be ready in fifteen minutes. Shall I bring it upstairs on a tray?'

'That's a good idea,' Alicia agreed. 'I'll show you the bedroom, Dev.'

He followed her up the stairs. He was rather silent, looking around as they climbed. Alicia told him about the house matter-of-factly. He didn't comment or ask any questions. She supposed he was very tired, but she wished that he showed some interest, now that they were here.

'This is the bedroom,' Alicia said finally, opening the door. 'Your bedroom,' she added hastily, and this time there was no glimmer of humour on his face. He looked curiously around the large, spacious room and walked over to the window to look down at the rose garden below. Several acres away he could see the woodline. 'It's beautiful,' he said over his shoulder. He sounded polite.

'Makes a change, doesn't it?' she agreed, smiling,

trying not to feel anxious. He nodded, moving from the window. He wandered to the bureau and picked up one after another of his personal articles from on top. Alicia set down his bag on the bed and began to unpack, as Dev opened one of the drawers, examining the contents.

'It's strange . . .' he said slowly, to no one in particular.

'I know, it must be.' She had had his things from the flat moved back. She didn't see any point in telling him about the separation. She glanced around the room. It looked like always, she thought, satisfied.

He went back to the picture window and sat down in one of the easy chairs, staring out.

'Shall I leave you for a while?' she asked tentatively. 'Would you like to be alone?'

'No,' he said glancing at her. 'No, stay. Tell me more about—us.' It was the first time he had made any direct reference to their marriage. Alicia said hesitantly:

'Maybe you'd better lie down for a while first?'

His eyes were weary. 'I've been lying down. For three months. Talk to me.'

She sat in the chair across from him, a little uneasy under that intent green gaze. She smoothed her skirt, saying casually, 'What would you like to know?' She had tried to stick to generalities, happy generalities. He couldn't know there had ever been trouble, but she was suddenly uneasy.

'How long were—have we been married?'

'This makes the seventh month. During four of which you were a willing participant.' She smiled, mischievously, and he responded with faint humour,

'I'm not unwilling now. You're very attractive.'

'Thank you!' It was ridiculous to blush, but she felt as though a stranger complimented her. A very attractive and mysterious stranger. It was an oddly titillating sensation.

'So,' he said absently, 'we were practically just-marrieds when I had the accident?' She wished he wouldn't pin down the details.

'Practically.'

His eyes narrowed thoughtfully. 'I hadn't realised it was such a whirlwind courtship.'

'We knew what we wanted.'

His eyes held hers as though he were probing for an answer to a question still unmasked.

'The house and—everything, must be yours?' he queried.

'Ours. Fifty-fifty. I've got the papers to prove it.'

'Yes, but,' he didn't answer her smile, 'they must have belonged to you first? I couldn't have had much money as an artist.'

She smiled, saying, deliberately teasing, 'That's right, you married me for my money.'

He grinned back, the old smile, charming and assured.

'What a waste!'

She laughed, relieved that was over, but was prevented answering by Mrs Larke's arrival. Mrs Larke set the laden tray before them, saying in a scolding tone to Dev, 'Now you eat every bite!'

'I'd be back in hospital if I ate every bite,' he protested, amused.

'And you, too, Mrs Rafferty! The pair of you look like an ad for charity: stop world hunger!'

Dev and Alicia exchanged laughing looks and Mrs Larke shook her head, frowning. 'Now, I'm serious. It looks bad for me, the two of you running around like skeletons, and my cooking for you! You want to get some meat on you.' She looked smugly down at her own ample self. 'You know, the heavier look is coming back into fashion.'

She left them and Dev murmured, 'What does Mr Larke look like?'

'Mrs Larke,' chuckled Alicia.

He sighed. 'That's what I thought. Well, I can see her point in my case; I do look a wreck. But you look fine to me. I like slender women.'

An idea occurred to Alicia. 'Dev, what *do* you remember?'

He shrugged, poking his fork without interest at the brisket of beef. 'Not much.'

'But you remember your personal tastes?'

'I do if I don't think about it. When I think about it, it slips away. If I just *feel*—' he shrugged again.

Alicia propped her chin thoughtfully. 'But nothing about us?'

'Sorry.' His eyes flicked up to hers briefly.

Alicia looked down at her plate, avoiding his eyes. 'Good beef, isn't it?'

'Mm.' He took another poke at his. Despite Mrs Larke's threats, he ate very little. When they had finished, Alicia told him briskly it was nap time and saw him over to the bed.

'Your medication,' she said, handing him the tablets and a glass of water.

He tossed the tablets in, swallowed the water and handed the glass back to Alicia. 'I thought I was out of hospital,' he complained. He lay back, stretching out on the smooth counterpane.

Alicia grinned. 'You'd be appalled at the list of instructions they gave me concerning you.' She spread the eiderdown over him. His cheek nestled against the softness in an unconscious movement, his lids lowered. 'I'll be next door if you need me,' Alicia said softly, moving towards the door.

'Alicia?'

She paused, looking at him. The green eyes studied her gravely.

'You're very kind. Thank you.'

She smiled faintly. 'You're welcome.'

After all, you couldn't blame someone for something they did not know they had done. Alicia sat in the adjoining bedroom which, at least for the time being, would be hers. She considered her own feelings dispassionately. They were somewhat perplexed. The only thing she was sure of, was that she did love Dev.

Of course he was not exactly Dev any more. He was, but he was different in key ways. He was still far from well, that could be part of the problem. But there were personality differences. There was no cynicism. Also he was much less guarded, the mocking defensiveness gone. She reflected that she was seeing Dev, the real Dev, stripped psychologically bare. It was a God-given opportunity to understand him.

She wanted him to recover. She honestly did; she didn't think she could have stood, half as calmly, having her past, her identity, wiped out. She wanted it because he so urgently did. But if his memory returned it would put an end to this delicate new relationship. There could be no cautious courtship. She would never know if he really loved *her* In the back of her mind, the pain, the doubt, would always be there.

Dr Wales had been confident that Dev would

regain at least partial memory, although Dev had not made any progress in over a month. When he was stronger he would probably begin to recall. That might be weeks, even months, Alicia thought hopefully—and was immediately ashamed.

There was this thought: he might never recover his memory, but he might never fall in love with her either. She pushed that idea away, but it lingered like an acid taste in her mouth.

CHAPTER EIGHT

ALICIA was up early the next morning, peeking into the next room to see Dev still sound asleep, and returning to her own room to shower. Once more, Alicia cautiously opened the door to the adjoining bedroom. In the shadowy quiet, Dev appeared to sleep on. With an eye on the still bed, she tiptoed over to the dresser and edged out a drawer, wincing as it squeaked. Dev stirred and lifted his head.

'Mm. Morning,' he said lazily, blinking across at her.

'I'm sorry!' Alicia apologised. 'This stupid drawer! I wanted you to sleep in.'

'I think I have. What time is it?' He rolled on to his side, the blankets twisting around his lean form, and propped his head on his hand.

'About ten-thirty. How did you sleep?' She came over to the far side of the bed, clothes in hand, seating herself on the edge.

'Like I was drugged—which is not surprising.' He smothered a yawn, blinking as he unself-consciously studied Alicia. He reminded her of a cat, one of those tough, haughty, battle-scarred alley cats. 'I feel badly about taking this room,' he remarked. 'After all, it's not as though I know the difference.'

'Oh, I don't mind,' Alicia assured him. 'This room is quieter,' she lied glibly. 'What would you like to do today?'

'Mm.' He lay flat and stretched luxuriously. 'That sounds great.'

'What does?' Alicia grinned. She'd have liked to stretch out beside him and hold him. She imagined running her fingers through the short, crisp curls, kissing the long, thin column of his throat. Firmly she clamped down on those thoughts, as Dev said indolently:

'To be able to choose what I want to do. I was so sick of that damned hospital—' he broke off, eyeing Alicia, saying suddenly, 'I like that colour on you.' He nodded at the chocolate silk of her bathrobe.

She laughed. 'I'm not surprised. You bought it for me. Well—how about breakfast? Do you feel like coming downstairs for it?'

'Hell, yes. I'm no invalid.' He sat up and rubbed his head briskly.

'All right then,' Alicia said, rising. 'And after breakfast, if you like, I'll show you around the old homestead.'

'Sounds great.' He sounded a little preoccupied. Her look was inquiring. He met it with that charming smile that gave nothing away.

'Do you remember where the dining room is?' she asked, for lack of something to say.

His eyebrows rose. 'I'm amnesiac, not feeble-minded,' he protested.

She shrugged apologetically, and went back to her own room to dress. She waited to go downstairs till she heard Dev leave his room. Hearing her door close farther along the hall, he paused, waiting for her, and they went down the tall, wide staircase together.

He had selected jeans, which fitted him far more loosely than they had before, and a rust-coloured sweater. Again Alicia reflected on how intriguing it was that people could forget their name, but still know what they liked to wear.

'Is that a picture of your sister on the dresser?' he asked, out of the blue.

There was a wedding portrait of Jacqueline and Victor in the master bedroom. Alicia had forgotten about it. 'That's Jacqueline,' she agreed.

'She doesn't look much like you. And I suppose the other portrait is of your Aunt Elizabeth?'

'Yes.' Alicia was still smarting over the 'doesn't look much like you.'

'Are you very close to them?'

Alicia considered it seriously. 'Not as close as I'd like to be,' she admitted. 'They're rather—self-sufficient people.'

He looked at her curiously. 'You're not?'

'I mean emotionally. Emotionally, they don't need a lot of demonstration—it's hard to explain.'

'No, I understand that.' Because he was like that himself? 'My parents were like that,' he added casually. 'Complete unto themselves.'

It came out so naturally, Alicia almost didn't notice till his hand shot out, reaching for the bannister, as though to stop himself from pitching forward.

'Dev!' she exclaimed in a mix of excitement and alarm. 'You remembered!'

He gave her a blank look, then his forehead wrinkled with concentration. 'Just for a minute,' he muttered, 'it was there, like a picture—' A fine sheen of perspiration beaded his upper lip, his eyes half shut, as though seeing into the distance.

'Don't try to force it!' Alicia charged, her hand catching his arm. He stared at her, his face tense, then slowly relaxed.

'No, you're right,' he agreed reluctantly. He didn't look too well, and she gazed at him with concern. His hand still gripping the bannister, he continued his descent, and Alicia followed helplessly. She had never been responsible for a sick person in her life; she was giving him his way, as she would a sick horse, letting him follow his instincts.

She was relieved to see that he seemed quite normal over breakfast, eating more than he had the night before, and brushing aside her suggestion that the grand tour could wait.

She showed him over the house they had picked together, and he was polite and interested, but absently so. Alicia guessed that he was testing his memory, seeking some recognisable anything to use as a keystone. The studio fascinated him. He went from painting to painting, examining every palate, easel, rag and brush. He stared out of the huge windows and finally shrugged hopelessly.

'Nothing. Not a damn thing,' he said frustratedly, looking at Alicia. 'This is supposed to be my life, but as far as I can tell—'

'Chromium oxide,' Alicia said.

'What?'

'What is chromium oxide?'

'Green paint,' he said, staring. 'So?'

'So? So you don't forget knowledge. You know how to read. You know how to paint. You don't know you know, that's all.'

'How comforting!' he exclaimed exasperatedly. 'I know, but I don't know!'

'The problem with you,' Alicia informed him, 'is that you're trying too hard. You're fighting all the time to remember and you're not ready. You have to relax. It's like when there's a word on the tip of your tongue. If you'd just forget about it—'

'No pun intended,' he put in drily.

'If you'd just stop *pushing*,' Alicia snapped, 'maybe your brain would have a chance.'

'That's easy for you to say,' he said impatiently. 'You're not the one who can't remember his own bloody name. You're not the one dependent on strangers for everything from food to your past!'

It hurt: 'stranger'. Understanding didn't erase the hurt. He saw her face and the anger died out of his. He said quietly, 'That was stupid. I'm sorry.' He hesitated, 'I'm very grateful—'

'I don't want your gratitude,' Alicia interrupted hotly. 'I don't want anything from you, believe it or not. I care about you, Dev. That's all. I don't expect anything back—I don't expect you to love me when you don't even know me. But we can be friends, can't we?'

'I'd like that,' he said. She couldn't tell from his tone whether he meant it or not.

'It's not fair to resent me!' she said fiercely.

'I don't,' he objected quickly.

'Knock, knock!' a voice said brightly behind them. They turned together to face Jacqueline, slenderly striking in a pale blue jumpsuit that picked up her eye colour. She smiled dazzlingly from the door.

'What are you doing here?' Alicia asked with more surprise than pleasure.

'I thought I'd drive out and visit. I didn't realise, till your Mrs Larke told me just a moment ago, Devereaux was home.' Her kiss on Alicia's cheek was brief, Dev's briefer. She studied him with curious eyes. 'How are you feeling, Dev? Glad to be home?'

'Fine, thanks—and yes, I am, very.' The direct look he gave Alicia brought reluctantly pleased colour to her cheeks.

*

'What did you think of Jacqueline?' Alicia inquired over dinner.

Dev hesitated. 'I think she's not overly fond of me,' he remarked. He took a long swallow of milk, watching Alicia curiously over the glass rim.

'No,' Alicia agreed uncomfortably. 'My family wanted me to marry someone like Victor—from their social strata.'

'Yours too,' he said thoughtfully. 'Why didn't you?'

'Boring,' Alicia said succinctly. 'Stuffy and artificial.'

He laughed. 'That's clear enough.'

'Jacqueline's beautiful, though isn't she?'

'Rather typical—' He broke off, putting his hand to his eyes. 'Déjà vu.'

'Dev—!' Alicia's voice was sharp with alarm. After a moment she rose, moving to his side.

He looked up frowning. 'I thought—for a minute I thought I remembered—having this conversation before.' He shut his eyes briefly, then opened them. 'It's gone!' he said impatiently. Unexpectedly he smiled faintly, taking in Alicia's blue eyes, wide with concern. 'Sorry! Did I scare you?' His breath was warm on her cheek, his lashes close enough to brush hers. 'You have to stop worrying,' he murmured, his eyes tracing her mouth.

Alicia straightened up, saying awkwardly, 'I know. Strong maternal instincts.'

'I don't think I see you as my mother,' he said, eyes tilting in amusement.

She smiled back, aware again of that magnetic bond of attraction between them.

'What do you see me as?' she asked innocently.

His eyes flickered. 'My sister?' he suggested blandly.

Alicia sighed with impatience at this teasing, then laughed reluctantly at the knowledgeable humour in his eyes. She returned to her chair, and they studied each other over the table like amiable fencing partners.

Somewhat to Alicia's frustration, their relationship remained platonic. They were good friends, but there was nothing lover-like in Dev's reactions to her, as far as Alicia could tell. Sometimes he flirted teasingly with her, but Alicia knew better than to take that seriously. She usually reacted dampeningly, making Dev grin.

The amnesia persisted, despite an occasional memory flash. Alicia spoke to Dr Andrews privately, after one of Dev's check-ups, but his answer was much the same as ever: patience, rest, peace. Those were the ingredients to a complete recovery.

'Of course,' he added thoughtfully, 'Devereaux may not want to remember.'

'Oh, but he does,' Alicia objected.

'Consciously, no doubt. But sometimes the subconscious works to protect one from remembering painful or frightening things—in cases of shock or trauma to the brain. If there were something Dev didn't wish to remember, then there is a possibility that his subconscious sabotages his efforts at recall.'

'If that were the case,' Alicia mused, 'would Dev ever remember?'

'Most likely. As he grows stronger there is less need for the self-defence mechanism. There is no physical reason Dev should not make a full recovery.'

*

'You were a long time,' Dev remarked as Alicia slid in behind the wheel and shut the car door. His eyes were curious, as Alicia glanced at him.

'Sorry,' she said absently.

'What were you talking about?'

'About the amnesia.'

'What about it?' he asked edgily, shifting in the seat.

'Just that—it was really nothing, Dev. I was just concerned that you still haven't recovered your memory. He was reassuring me that there's no physical reason you can't remember. It's a matter of patience and rest.'

He studied her intently. 'That's all?'

'That's all,' Alicia said off-handedly. 'But I was thinking it might be a good idea if we started pursuing our normal lives.'

'What does that mean?' Dev asked quietly.

'That I think I should go back to the Gallery. And I think you should start painting.'

He stared at her for a long moment before saying flatly, 'And if I can't—paint?'

'You won't know till you try.'

'For God's sake, don't sound so bloody preachy!' he said tautly. 'I'm not a child!'

'I realise that! But if you don't try—'

'You don't think I am going to remember, do you?' he said bitterly. 'That's what this is all about. You think I should get on with my life and not wait for my memory to return.' His eyes were hard and accusing.

'Dev, no! I promise you, it's not that!' And then, frustratedly, 'Would it be so terrible if you didn't?!'

He stared out the window, his jaw rigid.

'My God, it could be worse! You could be blind or paralysed! What is it with you? Am I so repugnant?'

'It has nothing to do with you!' he said tightly.

'Hasn't it?' Angrily she turned the switch in the ignition, starting the car.

They drove in silence till Dev reached over and switched on the radio. Classical music: sweet, lively violins filled the car's echoing silence.

Dinner was depressing. They both ate in a desultory fashion, their conversation stilted. At about nine, Dev wished her a toneless goodnight and went upstairs. Half an hour later Alicia followed him. Her room seemed empty and cold in the lamplight. She undressed, washed, put on her nightgown and climbed into bed.

She was nearly asleep when she heard the thud. It took several drowsy seconds for the sound to register. Her eyelids jerked open. That had come from Dev's room. She listened tautly. No further sound. She relaxed into the pillows. Then she thought: he's still on medication. If he woke and got up and was dizzy and fell—and hit his head . . . ? She threw aside the blankets, hurrying to the door, and jerked it open.

The room was dark but moonlit. In the silvery light she could see the bed, covers thrown back, empty.

'Dev!' she whispered, alarmed.

She saw out of the corner of her eye his shadowy movement. He was sitting in one of the chairs by the window, she realised in relief, as he said quietly, 'What's wrong?' His silhouette was etched in silver against the windows.

'I heard something like a crash,' she said softly, walking towards him. He sat back in the chair, and his face was lost in shadow.

'I knocked over the little table by that chair,' he said. 'Sorry.'

'What are you doing?' she asked, still softly.

'I couldn't sleep. I thought I'd sit up for a while.'

'You took your sedative, didn't you?' she asked quickly.

'No.' She stood next to him, looking down at his face, pure and cold in the moonlight. 'I'm sick of being sedated. I'm not an invalid.' He was probably sick of her nurse-maiding as well, but she continued to stand there.

'You know how vital it is that you rest properly,' she said slowly. She was very conscious of his lean maleness in the colourless silk of his pyjamas. She wished she dared to reach out and touch the remote masculine beauty of his face. His eyes looked strange and elfin in the silver wash of moonlight. They stared so intently up at her.

'Shall I get your pills?' she murmured.

'No. You people are turning me into a dope fiend.' He continued to stare and Alicia said hesitantly, 'Well, if you're all right, I guess I'll go back to bed.' But she remained where she stood, clenching her hands to keep from reaching out to him. He looked so far away in the sterile light, she wanted to reassure herself that he was really there.

'I'm sorry,' she said at random. 'About today.'

His eyes were like glass, she thought.

'Sorry?' He sounded blank.

'It's hard for me to understand how it must be for you,' she gave a small deprecating laugh, 'although you've explained it often enough. I guess I'm rather dense.'

His eyes flickered as he stared at her, not speaking. She turned and he said suddenly, softly, 'Alicia?'

'Hmm?'

He stood up and she was aware of him with greater

vividness than before, her nerves tightening. He was not an arm's length away, his scent filling her nostrils: warm and cleanly male. Her heart began to beat faster.

'What you said today—about my finding you repugnant; you don't believe that do you?'

'How about, just not attractive?' Alicia asked, trying to sound amused.

'You must be joking!' His hand reached out and his fingers touched her face lightly. 'You must know—' his voice dropped even more softly '—how beautiful you are.'

Alicia swallowed dumbly, shaking her head. His fingers brushed over her lips, her eyes, as though he were blind and seeking her. Her skin tingled responsively to his touch.

'But you are,' he whispered. 'You're one of the most beautiful women I've ever seen.'

You've forgotten the others, Alicia started to point out, but then his lips were touching hers in a gentle, exploratory kiss. She met his searching touch eagerly, the blood beginning to pound in her head.

Dev raised his head. 'Is this part of the therapy?' he muttered, his hands slipped down over her shoulders, his thumbs stroking her breast bone absently, waiting.

'Therapy?' gasped Alicia. 'What are you talking about?' She started to pull back, he held her still. 'I'm still rather a wreck, aren't I,' he murmured, 'and you're such a dutiful, devoted nurse.'

'Are you *crazy*?' Alicia cried. 'Dev, you're my husband.'

'No argument there.' His lips brushed hers again. For a moment she held herself stiff, but she had waited too long, she wanted him too much. She slipped her arms around his neck, pressing against him and touching his soft, wavy hair with caressing hands as she had longed to. With no apparent effort, Dev lifted her into his arms, carrying her to the bed.

Alicia kissed his face lightly. She could feel excitement building up within her as he settled her on cool sheets, lying beside her. Her limbs began to tremble. He gathered her more closely against him, his head bent, trailing fire across the valley between her breasts. Alicia's hands clutched his shoulders as he bent over her. She smoothed her hands up over his neck, locking behind his head.

'I've been so afraid,' she said softly. 'I thought you didn't want me.'

'Didn't want you,' he exclaimed amazedly. He smiled, she could feel his mouth move under her fingers. Then his head lowered and his mouth met hers with a heat that turned her bones liquidly with delight; a long, probing kiss. Her mouth parted sweetly, eagerly to his questing. Her body throbbed at his hungry insistence.

As his head raised reluctantly, Alicia gave a little sigh of satisfaction. Dev laughed softly, his lips teasing hers.

'Now here's something,' he said throatily, 'I remember how to do!'

Alicia turned her head cautiously to watch Dev sleep in the soft morning light. His supine body was a heavy welcome weight upon her arm. His face was peaceful. Alicia thought of last night and smiled a contented little smile.

Maybe it didn't answer everything, but it settled the question of whether he was attracted to her, that was a beginning, and everything had to begin somewhere. Dev stirred and Alicia slid her arm free into a more comfortable position. She nestled against him.

His eyes opened and he smiled sleepily. His arm slipped over her back and he rested his cheek upon her tousled hair. Listening to the slow steady pound of his heart beneath her ear, she sighed pleasurably. She doubted if there was another place on earth as warm and cosy.

'Morning,' Dev mumbled into her hair, drowsily.

Alicia chuckled softly. She felt alert and animated, but she lay quietly, enjoying his tranquillity.

'What's so funny?' Dev asked. His fingers tickled her side lightly.

'I'm just happy,' Alicia answered vaguely.

'Me, too.'

'Are you?' she asked quickly, wriggling on to her stomach, eyeing him hopefully.

The green eyes opened lazily. 'Mm-hmm.' His hand lifted and he brushed his knuckles against her cheek, caressingly. Outside the wind lashed a wave of rain against the bedroom window; they heard the pin-prick rattle.

'Is it raining?' Dev asked, raising his head slightly.

'Since dawn.'

'Let's stay in bed all day,' he suggested dreamily, shutting his eyes and sliding his other hand over Alicia's side.

'I can't. I promised Mr Maxwell I'd go in today,' Alicia said regretfully. A few minutes passed and she wondered if he were drowsing again, then he said reflectively, opening his eyes:

'For an independent woman, you have an awfully old-fashioned name, Alicia.' He smiled at her. 'I liked it the first time they told me about you.'

'Did you?' she said, doubtfully pleased.

'It suits you. It's different. Which reminds me: what does the inscription of my ring mean? Love's Good Fortune?'

She met his curious gaze, smiling shyly. 'It was an answer to people like my Aunt Elizabeth who thought—' she hesitated.

'Thought what?'

'That you married me for the money. It was saying that *I* was the fortunate one. To love you was *my* good fortune.'

His eyes tilted. 'That's sweet.' He kissed her ear. 'You're sweet.'

'I'm late,' she said mournfully, glancing at the clock. She sat up, sighing, and looked at Dev who folded his arms comfortably behind his head.

'Lazy! What are you going to do today?'

He said casually, watching her beneath half-lowered lids, 'I thought I'd try painting—'

'Oh, Dev!' She flung herself down on him and hugged him. 'Will you?'

He was laughing. 'I'm not promising anything,' he warned.

'I *know* it will work out,' Alicia certified. 'If you just try.'

'I promise to try,' he said mock solemnly.

'That's all that's necessary,' Alicia said, holding him tightly. 'That's all that's needed.'

The memory of last night kept Alicia smiling to herself all day. Everyone seemed nicer, the day less cold and gloomy because she had last night's memories tucked away in the back of her mind to be pulled out and examined every free moment. She tried to keep perspective; like Dev's return to the studio, it was a good sign but not a definitive answer. Nonetheless, she was happy.

When she returned home she dawdled in the kitchen for some time with Mrs Larke, who told her Dev had been in the studio all day.

'Shall I wait dinner?' Mrs Larke inquired as Alicia studied the refrigerator contents, and settled on a glass of milk and an apple.

'Not on my account,' Dev said from the doorway. 'I'm starving.'

Alicia straightened up, meeting the long, mocking look he sent with a suddenly trembly feeling in her legs. She was very conscious of Mrs Larke's all-knowing satisfied regard.

She cleared her throat. 'Hmm—how did it go today?' She said it casually. She didn't want to make a big deal of last night, because she knew that sex in itself didn't prove anything. She didn't want to look foolish.

'I missed you,' Dev said frankly, unperturbed by Mrs Larke's interested delight. Alicia swallowed.

'I missed you, too,' she mumbled gruffly. She would never be able to say things like that aloud, without self-awareness.

'So come and say hello,' Dev grinned. He turned his laughing look on Mrs Larke who shook her head, turning back to the vegetables she was scrubbing beneath the running tap. Dev reached Alicia and bent his head, grazing her lips lightly. He turned his head slightly, brushing her mouth back and forth with his.

'I believe you're shy,' he murmured.

'Dev,' she laughed a little protestingly. She was leaning her weight against him, weakly. That's all it took. A few light kisses and she was melting. Never mind that Mrs Larke was not ten feet away, never mind that she felt helpless and awkward, not knowing how he felt. With little or no encouragement she could fall back into the old pattern of defenceless yearning.

The knowledge dampened Alicia's instinctive response. She pulled away, smiling warily, and crunched into her apple. Her eyes met his and lowered shieldingly.

Dev cocked his head, his eyebrows wry.

He continued to watch her all evening with the same quizzical amusement. It made Alicia nervous. She realised that whatever advantage she had had was subtly changed, banished by the night before. She wasn't sure why exactly, but she sensed that his former tension regarding herself was resolved. He no longer made any attempt to keep her at a distance, there was no longer a comfortably detached friendship between them.

After last night, Alicia feared Dev would see her as she really was—the old Alicia: insecure, backward and hungry for love. When she pictured Dev falling in love with her it was an unreal, ideal Alicia she envisioned him falling for; the surface Alicia. She had hoped to have done away with the underneath Alicia by now, for she could never imagine Dev falling in love with herself as she was now.

These bits and pieces of confused thought drifted behind Alicia's cautious remarks and guarded expressions, while Dev continued to study her with his eyes amusedly tilting. It was maddeningly as though he knew exactly what was going on in her head.

'How did it go in the studio today?' she asked aggressively over the lemon fromage dessert, deciding to put him on the defence.

Dev licked his fork clean, reflectively holding it as though he were gauging perspective on her. 'Interesting,' he said non-committally. 'I think you're right about my trying too hard. Towards the end, when I relaxed and let it just happen—' He shrugged.

'That's good,' Alicia stated without particular interest, scooping up a forkful.

He smiled faintly, watching her. 'I suppose so.'

'Mr Maxwell can hardly contain himself till your next masterpiece.'

He was silent, measuring her tone. Alicia listened to its echo in her head and knew that she was behaving unreasonably. She laid her fork down and said unhappily, 'I've got an awful headache. I think I'll go straight to bed.'

He stood up and she added hastily, 'Oh, don't bother, please.' But he went to the door, holding it for her, and Alicia had to walk out past him, feeling his eyes in every nerve of her body. What must he be thinking of her?

'Goodnight, Alicia,' Dev said quietly. 'I hope you feel better in the morning.'

She mumbled a reply, and as the door shut behind her, ran across the hall and up the stairs to her bedroom. She felt like a fool. What on earth was the matter with her? She felt insecure and vulnerable and so she proceeded to behave like the worst gauche simpleton in the world?

She was still lying awake in bed when she heard Dev go into his room next door. She listened to the muffled sounds of his undressing and washing up. After a while the bar of light beneath the door vanished. Alicia held her breath, hoping he would open the adjoining door. Long minutes passed and

her hope slowly died. She had spoilt everything with
her fears.

The next day, Alicia felt even more awkward,
constrained by Dev's polite distance. She was reminded of the terrible period before their separation.
The similarity filled her with sick fear. She couldn't
go through that again. She had started this, somehow she would have to stop it.

Yet each time she brought herself to the point of
speech, Dev's cool, austere profile, half buried in the
morning paper, drained her courage. After work, she
decided, and left for the Gallery trying to look as
though she had forgotten to kiss Dev, in the rush, and
not that she was avoiding it.

The day dragged on for ever. When it finally
ended, she was further frustrated by the memory
that it was Tuesday, and every Tuesday she visited
Aunt Elizabeth. She could call and cancel, of course,
but it would only make the next visit more unpleasant. Reluctantly Alicia reversed directions, and
headed back to her aunt's.

Aunt Elizabeth was in a dour mood. The rainy
weather played up her arthritis, and kept her friend
Lady Coolidge from their bridge game.

'You know, Alicia,' her aunt said pointedly, 'you
could sit in for Elsinore.'

Alicia nearly choked on her cucumber sandwich.
'I'm terrible at bridge,' she reminded her aunt quickly. 'Remember how irritated you get when I play?'

Aunt Elizabeth gave her a quelling eye. 'It wants
concentration, which you lack. I think it would be
good for you to play occasionally.' She sipped her
tea.

'It's nice of you to ask,' Alicia replied, 'but I really
can't. Dev—'

'I'm sure you could call Devereaux and explain,' Aunt Elizabeth broke in. 'You certainly owe him nothing more.'

Sidetracked, Alicia said with slight impatience, 'Dev is still my husband, Aunt Elizabeth.'

Her aunt's haughty brows rose slightly. 'You really haven't changed a bit, have you? Outwardly, of course, but inside you're the same sentimental muddlehead.'

Alicia laughed shortly, putting down her cup with a click. 'Yes,' she said clearly, 'I am. You may as well accept it. I'm not going to change.' She recognised the flat truth with surprise. Accept it, she thought grimly. You are what you are. If you don't like yourself, no one else will either.

'It's nothing to be proud of,' Aunt Elizabeth informed her. 'You've made a mess of your private life, everyone knows. That man—'

'All right!' yelled Alicia, getting to her feet. Aunt Elizabeth's dignified features mirrored astonishment, her hand froze, the tea cup halfway to her mouth.

'Now listen,' Alicia snapped. 'I appreciate that you have always tried to be a proper guardian. And I realise that I have always been a big disappointment to you. But you have Jacqueline, and she's a perfect Carrington, so you ought to be satisfied with that and stop regretting that I'm not what you wanted, because I'm here to stay. And Dev is here to stay—I hope—because I love him, and I need him, and he matters more to me than anything or anyone else. I know he's not perfect and I know you don't like him, but if you care about me at all—if you care about continuing a relationship with me—than you won't criticise him any more!'

Aunt Elizabeth set her cup down. 'My dear girl,' she said stiffly, 'there is no need for hysteria. You misunderstand my concern. However, in future, if you're going to be so sensitive, I will refrain from— giving my opinion of your unfortunate husband.'

It was Alicia's turn to be amazed. She had expected Aunt Elizabeth to go through the roof, instead she had practically backed down. It suddenly occurred to Alicia, musing over her aunt's stark reaction to Dev, to wonder whether Aunt Elizabeth had ever had to sacrifice her happiness to family pride. It would explain so much that had puzzled and hurt Alicia, but she knew too that never would Aunt Elizabeth be brought to discuss such a subject.

With unexpected insight, Alicia realised that her aunt genuinely did care for her, in her own way, and did not want to lose her. Like everyone else, Aunt Elizabeth needed affection as well as respect; she just couldn't admit it. It was as though a magic spell had been lifted, a curse broken. She need never fear Aunt Elizabeth again—not because she had her own life now, but because there was nothing really to fear in Aunt Elizabeth. There never had been. The thing Alicia had feared had been in herself all along.

Alicia sat down again to finish her tea, feeling indescribably relieved. She glanced surreptitiously at her aunt, who gave her a suspicious look, and bit primly into another cucumber sandwich.

She was a little late arriving home for dinner. Dev met her at the front door.

'*Where* have you been?' he demanded, taking her raincoat from her, and dropping it absently over a chair-back. His eyes were bright and angry. Alicia blinked at him, surprised. It was so out of character.

'I went to see my aunt,' she answered.

'For three and a half hours?'

'Well, yes.'

'Without calling?'

'I thought you would remember. You know I go on Tuesdays to see her,' objected Alicia. She felt a tiny twinge of gratification that he had been worried by her lateness.

'Not for three and a half hours you don't!' His eyes raked over her, still hard. 'I didn't know what the hell had happened to you!'

'You could have phoned Aunt Elizabeth's,' she pointed out.

'Really? And if you hadn't been there? She'd have loved that!' It was the first sign of any annoyance or resentment he felt towards her family's attitude about their marriage. He must be very angry for it to slip out like that. Alicia studied him uncertainly.

'Well, where else would I be?' she inquired reasonably.

'Who the hell knows, the way you've been acting lately!'

To give herself time to think, she picked her coat up, shaking it and moving to hang it in the hall closet.

'Don't turn your back on me!' he bit out, and grabbed her arm, turning her to face him.

'Dev—' Alicia expostulated, disbelieving. She blinked up, taking in the hard line of his mouth and the temper gleaming in his eyes. A nervous laugh escaped her.

Dev swore, glaring at her, his eyes going dangerously dark. Then, abruptly, his lips twitched. He gave a reluctant laugh. 'Damn you, Alicia,' he growled, shaking her a little. 'Don't do that again!' His fingers relaxed their pinching grip.

'I'm sorry,' Alicia apologised. She wasn't sure exactly what not to do again: be late? turn her back? laugh? She couldn't control her mischievous smile. She wanted him to forget his irritation. She had missed him, she was glad to be home. She wanted to erase yesterday.

Dev's arm slipped around her waist, giving her a little squeeze. 'Then how was Aunt Elizabeth?' he asked, as they walked into the sitting room. His temper had vanished as though it had never been. He seemed as eager as she to forget yesterday's strain 'And what will you have to drink?' He walked towards the drinks' trolley.

'Fine and a sherry, please.' She missed the warmth of his hand through the thin silk of her blouse. She sank down into one of the comfortable leather chairs, watching him pour their drinks. 'How did it go in the studio today?' she queried, smoothing her skirt.

'I remembered something today,' he offered over his shoulder. He placed the stopper back in the decanter.

Alicia looked up quickly. 'Did you?' She heard the wariness in her voice.

Dev didn't seem to notice, bringing her sherry to her and dropping his lean length into the sofa across from her.

'Fragments,' Dev was saying, unaware of her unease. 'At first I didn't even notice I was remembering, it happened so naturally.' He was so much stronger, so much more cheerful and optimistic, it was inevitable that his memory should soon return. She had best prepare herself.

'What did you remember?' she questioned carefully, watching his face.

His smile was faint. 'Nothing earth-shaking, or

even very interesting, I'm afraid, except to me; stuff about painting mostly. Some things about school, too, a long time ago.' He sipped his wine.

'Nothing about us?' Alicia pressed. 'About me?'

He shook his head, his expression regretful. 'Nothing. The last few years are as big a blank as ever—except for the painting: *that's* coming back.' She heard the satisfaction in his tone. She was glad for his sake, she was more relieved, however, that it wasn't anything to do with them.

'You know, I was thinking today—' he began meditatively, then he glanced at Alicia and left the thought trailing unfinished. She didn't pursue it, instinctively alerted by his tone, for coming trouble.

She didn't know what the trouble was till later that night, when they lay in bed, listening to the rain drum down on the roof.

'I want to paint you,' Dev said lazily, his hand stroking her hair lightly. Instantly Alicia's drowsy peace dissolved, as though cold water had poured down on her. For a moment she didn't answer. Then she mumbled, without particular tact, '*Why?*'

'Because you're beautiful.'

'No, I'm not,' she said almost grumpily. She didn't want him painting her, she wasn't sure why. Because it could trigger the wrong kind of memories?

He laughed, discounting her objection. 'Then because you're available?' he suggested.

She gave a little snort then sighed, moving her cheek against his smooth, warm chest. His arms nestled her closer.

'My little hedgehog,' he murmured.

'What?'

Dimly, she saw his teeth flash in a quick smile. 'All

prickly insecurity and bristly caution, but underneath, all soft and sweet and warm. Hmm?'

She didn't know what to answer.

'I wonder why?' he added, reflectively.

Dev continued to make steady progress in his recovery. He was gradually regaining his weight, and his
face recovered its healthy colour. His hair grew
quickly and, by February, there were no outward
physical signs of his accident. Dr Andrews had given
him a clean bill of health on his last visit. He had a
resilient constitution, but he was highly strung. The
rapid completion of his physical recovery, Dr
Andrews had no doubt, was due to Alicia. Alicia
didn't know what Dev could have said to implant
this notion. Her own opinion was that the tranquillity of home and Mrs Larke's excellent cooking were
responsible for putting Dev back on his feet so soon.

There were occasional nervous headaches. Dr
Andrews theorised that these arose from Dev's
pushing to remember what his subconscious preferred to withhold. Stubbornly he kept prying, pulling
bits and scraps out into his conscious. He listened
politely to Dr Andrew's advice about relaxing, and
continued to stretch and test his memory. Reluctantly, the protective grip of his subconscious was loosen-
ing. The sketchy framework of his past was fleshing
out. The one exception was the past year. That
remained a complete and total blank. It was shoving
at this mental door that gave Dev headaches and left
him frustrated.

CHAPTER NINE

'How are you these days?' Jacqueline sipped her white wine, giving Alicia an inquiring look. They were lunching at a small French restaurant Jacqueline frequented. 'We don't see much of you,' she continued.

'I keep busy,' Alicia said off-handedly, selecting some shrimp pâté. 'Exercising the horses—'

'And Dev?' Jacqueline asked, following the pâté's trip from the tray to Alicia's mouth with her eyes. 'How's Devereaux?'

'He's fine,' Alicia said a little thickly.

'He's painting again?'

'Mmm.'

Jacqueline watched her take another portion of pâté. She sighed. 'Has he regained his memory yet?'

'Most of it.' Alicia glanced at her sister. Jacqueline looked the picture of beautiful preoccupation in a brown silk dress, nibbling absently on one long, red-lacquered fingernail. 'You ought to try some of this,' Alicia told her. 'It's delicious.'

'I've got to watch my weight,' Jacqueline said absently. 'I'm pregnant.'

Alicia straightened up in her seat. 'Jacqueline, that's wonderful!' she exclaimed. 'When?'

'October.' Her sister smiled a little at Alicia's enthusiasm.

'Aren't you excited?' Alicia demanded.

Jacqueline shrugged. 'Of course. But I'm not looking forward to the next seven months, I can tell you.' Her gaze moved regretfully to the pâté and then away.

'Does Aunt Elizabeth know?' Alicia asked.

'Of course.' She gave Alicia a tolerant look. 'You're such a sentimentalist. Having babies is no big deal. Any moron can do it.'

'Actually this lunch isn't without motive,' Jacqueline went on, clasping her hands on the table. 'Victor wants me to have my portrait painted now—radiant motherhood, and all that. He wants Dev to do it.'

'*Dev?*' Alicia repeated, disbelievingly. 'Why? Victor doesn't like Dev.'

'Oh—' Jacqueline brushed that aside as silly. 'Victor did some checking up. You know, the Lambs have one of Devereaux's paintings, and so do the Crichtons. Your husband is somebody to be reckoned with in art circles, isn't he? Victor was quite impressed.'

'I think I see,' Alicia said with unaccustomed dryness.

Jacqueline smiled her dazzling, pointed smile. 'It's only natural we should want the best, and if we can keep it in the family, so much the better. Anyway, you'll talk to Dev and see what he thinks of the idea?'

'Oh, sure,' Alicia said without expression. She already knew what *she* thought of the idea. Dev spending day after day painting Jacqueline's lovely face, confronted with Jacqueline's charm and wit? No thank you!

'Well then, that's settled,' Jacqueline said in businesslike tones. She nodded to the distantly hovering waiter. 'Let's order.'

*

Dev was upstairs in the studio when Alicia arrived home. She went straight up and found him applying the finishing touches to a painting he was doing of the studio view of the woods. It was very good, almost an aerial view with a whimsical suggestion of glass and windowsill. The woods were tantalising with their look of early spring, like water just out of reach.

Alicia sighed to herself watching Dev's absorbed face. He wore his favourite painting shirt, a paint-daubed olive denim, sleeves rolled to the elbows, tucked casually into faded levis. His clever fingers flicked over the canvas.

She knocked softly on the door frame and he straightened with a jerk, glancing in her direction impatiently. His eyes lightened taking in Alicia; he smiled that half-wicked, half-sweet smile that always made her heart pause mid-beat.

'I didn't hear the car.' He tossed down the brush and walked towards her, wiping his hands on a rainbow-streaked rag. Alicia's head tilted to meet his kiss. His lips were firm and warm, and in no hurry. But how long before his kisses became merely routine pecks?

Dev raised his head and smiled, studying her face. 'Bad day?'

'No,' she assured quickly.

'Come and see,' he told her, and guided her to the easel, his arm warm about her shoulders. He looked down inquiringly.

'Nice view,' she said mischievously. He gave her a pretend-fierce squeeze. 'All those years of study, and your expert opinion is "nice view"?' He grinned. 'Then that's what we'll title it.' He was always doing that, taking whatever idiotic first words left her and titling his paintings with them. It had become a game, the kind of game one played with children, reflected Alicia.

She turned away from 'Nice View' and left the circle of Devereaux's arm, walking to the window. 'I had lunch today with Jacqueline,' she said over her shoulder. She put her hands on her hips and rocked back on her heels, waiting, like a little boy, for a reaction. 'She wants you to paint her portrait.'

'I'd rather paint yours,' he said, coming up behind and slipping his arms around her waist. He locked his hands over her stomach and pulled her back against him. This was a small bone of contention: Alicia's sudden decision that she no longer wanted to be painted by him. She couldn't explain her reluctance, and even if she could, he would probably have just laughed it off. Instead she argued that she didn't have time, that she hated posing, that two portraits of one person were enough for posterity to handle.

Alicia laughed a little unsteadily. 'Well, she's pregnant now and Victor wants a Madonna masterpiece to hang over the front hall fireplace.'

He rested his cheek against the top of her head. After a moment he inquired, 'Would you like me to paint her?'

Alicia struggled briefly with herself and said in a cheerful tone, 'Yes, I think it would be a nice gesture. And it's good publicity for you.'

'I'm not a society painter,' he said briefly, lifting his head from her hair. He was silent, thinking, then he said lightly, 'Well, I'll strike a bargain. I'll paint your sister if you let me paint you as well.' What was his compulsion to paint her all the time? She had just offered him a beautiful, fresh model. Alicia shut her eyes for a second. It would be heaven on earth if she could relax and *believe* that he loved her. But she was terrified of being a fool twice, of ever again mistaking kindness and affection—even physical desire—for love.

'You can paint me any time,' she argued with an attempt at levity. 'Jacqueline won't be pregnant for ever.'

'That's the deal,' he said firmly. 'Both of you, or neither.'

Terrific, so she could be compared daily to Jacqueline? She took a deep breath. 'I guess that's fair.'

His laugh was a little short. 'Your enthusiasm is overwhelming.'

'You've painted me already,' Alicia explained uncertainly.

'Not that I recall.'

'Oh,' she hunched her shoulder against the faint humour in his tone.

'Were you this difficult a subject the first time?' He dropped a quick kiss on her shoulder.

'No, I—' she broke off. She didn't want to talk about then. She said at random, 'There's a message for you downstairs. A Dr Leidon called.'

'Oh?'

'Who's Dr Leidon?' Alicia tilted her head to see his face. Dev looked quizzical.

'He's a hypnotist. Rather famous.'

'A *hypnotist*?' Alicia said weakly. She turned to face him, trying to conceal her alarm. 'Why?'

'Nothing else has worked, I thought I might try hypnotism. They've had some great results—'

'No!' She pulled out of his arms.

Devereaux's green eyes narrowed, taking in her obvious agitation. He slowly shoved his hands in the levi pockets, waiting.

'I *mean*,' Alicia said, trying to cover with a smile, 'hypnotism is so—unscientific. Shouldn't you ask Dr Andrews?'

'I have. He approved.'

'But *why*?' Alicia protested.

After a long moment, Dev said without expression, 'I get the feeling you don't want me to get my memory back.'

'It's not that,' Alicia said hastily, 'and anyway, you are getting your memory back. You've got it back! Or enough of it!'

'Enough?' he iterated disbelievingly. 'Enough for whom? It's my life that's missing the big chunk!' Alicia whirled away to face the window. 'What is it you're afraid of?' he asked more calmly.

'Nothing!'

'Yes, you are. I've felt it before. You don't want me to remember. Oh, I know,' he forestalled her indignant turn towards him, 'not everything, just what concerns us. Why?'

'You're wrong.'

He rubbed his thumb meditatively against the side of his nose, studying her. Alicia's eyes fell, she moved away from him, clasping her arms around herself defensively.

'Dev,' she said in a low voice, 'I've never asked you for anything, but would you please, please not use hypnosis to regain your memory?'

'Alicia!' he exclaimed exasperatedly.

'*Please*, I promise I'll never ask for anything else as long as I live—'

'Alicia.' He moved to her and pulled her against him, as one would comfort a child. 'You can ask anything you like, but this is rather different—'

'It's not that I don't want you to remember,'

Alicia pleaded muffledly into his shoulder. 'Just to remember naturally, on your own.'

Dev sighed. 'All right—if it matters so. But it would be a hell of a lot simpler if you'd just tell me what you're so afraid of.'

'It's not anything like that,' Alicia said tiredly, and as he didn't reply, perhaps he believed her.

It had seemed so easy before, Alicia thought that night, brushing the heavy, raw silk of her hair. All she had to do was make him fall in love with her so that she could forgive and forget the first time, and they could get on with their life. But he hadn't fallen in love with her, and even if he did, getting his memory back could easily change everything. He might not forgive her.

The bathroom door swung open. Dev stood in his dressing gown, towelling dry his hair. 'You know,' he said, 'we ought to think about children.'

Alicia looked up, blinking. She caught her open mouth in the mirror and shut it. 'You mean *our* children?'

'Mm.' He came out, still briskly rubbing his hair. 'We didn't decide against having any?'

'We never talked about it.' She swivelled to watch him. He went back to the shower and came out a moment later without the towel. His hair gleamed with reddish glints, waving damply.

'I'd like a kid or two,' he remarked. He slipped off the dressing gown and got into the bed. Leaning on his side, his head propped, watching her, he added, 'You'd make a splendid mother.'

'Me?' Alicia said sceptically. She glanced at her reflection: at the wide blue eyes, the broad bones and wide childish plains, the full, sensitive mouth.

'That's a big responsibility,' she said to herself.

'You're a responsible person. And gentle and patient and imaginative. Those are important things in a mother. You'd like a child, wouldn't you?'

'Yes.' She would like a child, especially Dev's child. She figured Dev would make a good father: funny and tender and perceptive. The mental picture she conjured almost hurt in its sweet poignancy.

'Not that it isn't nice having you all to myself,' he added rather wickedly, still watching her.

Alicia laughed, rising and crossing over to the bed. She sat on the edge and Dev pulled her back against him. His mouth found hers with unexpected hunger, his arms pulled her possessively close.

Say it, Alicia thought urgently, *say that you love me. Tell me it's true.* Dev raised his lips and rubbed his face against hers, as though savouring its velvet smoothness. 'Either way,' he whispered, 'I don't think I can lose.' He reached up and snapped off the table lamp.

Dev was very careful with her in the studio, Alicia noticed, touched. Very patient, very considerate, very low-keyed. He was making a concentrated effort not to do anything to tense her up. He wasn't sure what made her so dislike sitting, but he was doing his best not to reinforce her dislike, and Alicia felt guilty about being so difficult.

She watched his face while he sketched, chatting absently to her. He was concentrating, but he was not absorbed by the work, she realised. Some of his attention was on her, gauging her mood, alert to any warning signs. His fingers scratched away in quick, delicate strokes.

'We should have eaten lunch in the woods today,' he was saying. 'Filled a basket and gone.'

'We could do that tomorrow,' Alicia suggested, in case he was serious.

'Let's.' He looked up, his fingers still moving, his eyes observant. 'What's that poem by Hardy? "Under the Waterfall"?'

Alicia tried to think of what poem he meant.

Dev quoted:

'And we placed our basket of fruit and wine,
by the runlet's rim, where we sat to dine.'

'Is that the one where he drops the wine goblet under the waterfall?' she inquired, enlightened.

'She.

"No lip has touched it since his and mine
In turns therefrom sipped lover's wine."'

He grinned at her wickedly.

Alicia knew the poem he meant, but she didn't see the connection. There was little similarity between Hardy's lovers' tryst and picnicking with Dev. She sighed restlessly and he immediately put down the sketch pad.

'That's enough for today,' he said briskly.

'Oh, I'm not tired,' she certified hastily.

'I am,' he said cheerfully. 'Let's have our tea. All this talk of picnics is making me hungry.'

He had a healthy appetite. Alicia like watching him put food away—where he put it was a mystery; he was all lean, graceful height.

She looked forward to tomorrow's picnic. She would stuff the heavy wooden basket with cheese and fruit and wine, cakes and little sandwiches with delectable fillings. She would bring along a wine glass too, just one. Then she thought that over and decided against it. She didn't want to embarrass Dev by appearing to think he had likened *them* to Hardy's lovers. She would bring two wine glasses, that was romantic enough for them.

'What are you frowning at?' Dev asked. 'Did you want that last tart?' He gave her a quizzical look.

She laughed. 'No! Not half as much as you did.' She decided to liven up. She didn't want to get all broody. He watched her carefully enough already. That speculative look made her nervous.

Jacqueline and Victor were to dine with them that evening and when they arrived they brought an unexpected present.

'Surprise, surprise,' Jacqueline said brightly, pushing a large beribboned box into Alicia's arms, and giving her a cool peck on her cheek. Dev and Victor shook hands briefly.

Alicia cautiously removed the box lid. A small black Labrador puppy blinked up at her and yawned a wide pink yawn. 'Dev!' she exclaimed delightedly, offering the box.

'I rashly told Anne Crichton I wanted one of her Tasha's first litter,' Jacqueline said, handing Dev her black fur coat. 'Anne took me seriously. She's had all her shots and naturally she's pure-bred—with papers.'

'Anne?' Dev inquired smoothly.

Jacqueline gave him a reproving look.

'Cute little beggar,' Victor said cheerfully, with a cursory glance at the box. 'I should watch that,' he added, as Dev lifted the puppy out. 'Not house-broken, you know.'

'I knew you'd find room for her,' Jacqueline said, watching Dev. 'Alicia was always mad for bringing strays home.'

He gave her a dry look, and knelt, setting the puppy on the highly polished floor. It waddled past

Victor's Italian leather shod feet, towards Alicia, who squatted down.

'Are you sure you don't want her?' she asked Jacqueline, cupping the puppy's face in her hand. 'Dogs and children go together—'

'One's enough to contend with,' Jacqueline informed her. 'And since I'm already stuck with the latter—' She leaned against Victor's arm, looking anything but Madonna-like in a sleek black strapless. Alicia felt underdressed in a blue silk kaftan. She looked at Dev who was observing his in-laws rather ironically. Meeting Alicia's eye he grinned faintly, and her spirits rose.

All in all it was a typical Jacqueline and Victor evening. Not precisely entertaining; as couples, even as individuals, Alicia and Dev shared little in common with Jacqueline and Victor. But it was as interesting as an evening can be when the topics of conversation are limited, and verged on fencing matches between Dev and Jacqueline.

'Maybe we should entertain more?' Alicia suggested later, after Jacqueline and Victor had gone and she and Dev had retired upstairs.

She was giving her hair its nightly brushing, watching Dev play with the puppy on the thick cream-coloured rug before the fireplace.

'Mm?' Dev said absently. He rolled the wriggling puppy over with a lean brown hand and tickled its fat little belly.

'Well,' reflected Alicia, 'we are a little isolated.'

Dev looked up. 'I didn't know you felt isolated.' He closed his fingers over the puppy's muzzle. It squirmed frantically. Dev continued to watch Alicia, his eyes serious.

'I was thinking more of you,' she said hesitantly.

'Me?' He cocked his brows. 'I'm not complaining. I've got everything I need right here.'

Alicia turned to conceal her pleasure, setting the brush on the dressing table tray. She walked over to join him on the rug, staring down at the puppy.

'What shall we name her?' she asked. 'She ought to have a special name, poor little orphan.'

'How about Rat?' Dev suggested. He tilted his head examining the twisting puppy. 'She looks like a rat, with her ears spread like that.'

Alicia chuckled. 'She needs something she can grow into. Look at those paws.'

'Fang?' Dev considered, ruefully examining his dented finger. 'Jaws?'

'She must be teething.'

'Nope. She's got her teeth.' He looked at Alicia, smiling. 'You looked very beautiful tonight. All cool and silky.' He put the puppy in its basket and it blinked at them surprised, as Dev stood up, pulling Alicia towards him.

'As beautiful as Jacqueline?' Alicia inquired, smiling slightly.

'No comparison.' He kissed her forehead and Alicia raised her lips receptively, pushing aside the regret that he could never mean what she wished he did.

CHAPTER TEN

'SOMEBODY tried to pick me up today!'

Dev looked up from Alicia's half surprised, half jubilant face to where Pudgy, also known as Panther, gnawed happily on one of Dev's old deck shoes. 'Look at her flaunt it in my face,' he remarked, and Pudgy looked up, cocking her ears intelligently.

'Well?' Alicia grinned cheekily. She drifted over to Jacqueline's half-finished portrait and inspected it. 'This is coming along,' she opined.

'Thanks. So what happened?'

She gave him an innocent look, which he met drily. Alicia laughed a little. 'Nothing very exciting. To tell you the truth, I barely noticed him. He was there quite a while, browsing, you know, and he caught my eye a few times and I smiled—just politely. Then he came over and we talked for a bit and he asked me to lunch.'

Dev put his hand on his hip, giving her an exasperated glance, and Alicia added hastily, 'which I declined.'

'I should hope so. Did you mention you were married?'

'Of course.' She turned back to the portrait, studying it critically. 'I don't think Jacqueline's going to like this,' she said after a moment.

It was very good; Jacqueline looked very lovely. Dev had placed her against a blue-grey background, standing half turned to the observer. Her daffodil off-the-shoulder dress was at odds with the arm curving protectively along the gentle swell of her belly. The charcoaled-in face had a sulky, almost bored look.

'Yes, she will,' Dev said carelessly. 'She looks sexy, and that's what she wants to feel now.'

'What are you doing?' he asked, coming into their room later. Alicia was lying on the bed, absently patting Pudgy, curled beside her, and flipping with her other hand through a large photo album.

'Showing Pudgy our honeymoon pictures,' she informed him, glancing up.

Dev sat down on the edge of the bed and Pudgy got up, climbing on to the photo album to go to him. She sat down on the slick open page, her stubby tail wagging as he caressed her briefly.

'Daddy's girl,' grumbled Alicia. She slid the puppy off the page, turning it.

'Weighing Hawaii against the might-have-beens?'

She looked up, uncomprehending. His tone was mocking, the tilted eyes curious.

'Huh?' Alicia asked brightly, screwing her forehead up.

'Don't you sometimes regret getting married so young?' Did he?

She shrugged.

A moment passed and he said so abruptly that she jumped, and Pudgy lowered her ears, 'Does it happen often?'

'Does what happen often?' Alicia asked blankly.

'Funny.' His look was unamused. Alicia's bewilderment increased. 'At work. Do guys try to pick you up often?' he repeated testily.

Alicia's mouth dropped and she laughed. It was the last thing in the world she would have expected:

Dev jealous of *her*? At her laughter, his eyes narrowed dangerously, and Alicia put her fist up nervously, to hide her quivering lips.

'Not half as often as you'd think,' she got out, unsteadily. The idea of men thronging to seduce her made it hard not to giggle.

He stood up and, to her disbelieving wonder, he was actually angry. He gave her a long, warning look, and left the room, slamming the door behind him with a violence that shook the walls.

Alicia jumped and started to laugh a little hysterically. Pudgy bumped her face inquiringly with her small, blunt head.

That night Dev made love to her with an energetic thoroughness that left Alicia limp. His hands were less gentle than demanding, his mouth hot and hungry. She sensed beneath his passion there still ran a thread of anger, although he had made no further mention of the incident upstairs when she had come down for dinner.

'Dev,' she protested, when he turned to her again, after they had rested for a little while. Roughly his mouth silenced her objections, his hands ruthlessly moving over her, forcing her to respond. She couldn't have resisted if she had wanted to, and she didn't. His passion was alarming, but it was thrilling too. She responded sweetly, her body moulding to his, responding eagerly to his demands. The silent intensity, the fierceness of their union, left her feeling scorched, sapped afterwards. Dev lay against her, one long leg sprawled across hers, one arm clasping her possessively tight, even in sleep. What was jealousy but pride of ownership, she thought scornfully of her own delight later. All the same, there was something satisfying in it.

Jacqueline made an impatient model. Alicia tried to stay out of the studio on the days Dev painted her sister, for the two invariably quarrelled and Alicia didn't want to be dragged into the middle.

'I used to think maybe you might prefer a woman with a livelier temperament,' Alicia told him softly one night, after a particularly stormy day.

Dev lay against her, his body heavy with the released tension of their lovemaking, his head pillowed against her. He snorted sleepily.

'Lively? How about vicious?'

Alicia stroked her hand down his long, lean back.

'You know,' she explained.

'I know I need—' he paused, searching idly for the word, 'haven'.

She had never thought of it that way before. Never thought that she, gentle and calm, might be more suited to his nature than someone as restless and variable as himself.

'Dev,' she began slowly, 'do you find me—boring?'

He laughed with genuine amusement. His hand slid down over her flat stomach to her hips. Alicia's breath caught with pleasure at his teasing fingers.

'Does it feel like I find you boring?' he asked lazily.

The following day, Dev came to the Gallery to take Alicia to lunch. He arrived without warning, causing a minor stir in the front lobby, and hunted Alicia out where she was waiting patiently with a prospective American buyer.

'Dev!' she exclaimed amazed, before guiltily lowering her voice as he sauntered up, graceful and cool, to join them. 'What are you doing here?'

'I've come to abduct you.' He tilted his head and

gave her a swift, sure kiss that left Alicia breathless and shy under the offended gaze of the client. Dev nodded at him pleasantly.

'Mr Denninger,' Alicia said weakly, 'may I introduce my husband, Devereaux Rafferty?'

The buyer's face changed. '*The* Rafferty?' he repeated alertly. Dev's eyebrows rose questioningly.

'Dev,' Alicia broke in, 'why are you here?'

'It suddenly occurred to me that I *hate* to eat alone—' he was beginning in a disarming tone, when—

'Devereaux, my boy!' Mr Maxwell called delightedly, and hurried up to join them. He and Dev shook hands.

'Oscar, you won't mind if I borrow Alicia for a bit?' Dev requested, with his charming smile.

'Take her!' Mr Maxwell gave Alicia away with a sweeping hand. 'Take the rest of the day, my dears.'

'Dev—' Alicia protested, half laughing.

He grinned, unrepentant. 'Made another date, did you?' he quizzed and she laughed, shaking her head. 'Then go get your purse. I'm starving.'

'I'm paying?' she teased. '*Now* I understand.'

The men laughed and Alicia nipped off to get her things. When she returned a moment later, a fourth person had joined the group. Alicia's heart stopped. She took in the tiny, petite figure in the black coolie pants and Chinese print blouse; the sleek dark hair and lovely pointed face: Magda.

Alicia started walking again. She reached the others, and stood between Mr Maxwell and Mr Denninger, facing Dev and Magda as though they were players on an opposing team.

Magda raised her eyebrows delicately. 'Alicia! Long time no see.' She looked absolutely unchanged.

And why not? It had only been a year. A traumatic and moulding year for Alicia; even Dev had changed. But not Magda. Magda looked across at Alicia with cool, scornful eyes, her mouth twisting in a small smile.

'Ready?' Alicia asked Dev in a hard, unfamiliar voice. 'Or else,' said her tone.

Dev blinked. Maxwell and Denninger exchanged glances. Alicia felt herself going red with embarrassed tension, and her grip tightened on her bag. Magda's violet eyes half closed in anticipation of Dev's reaction.

'Sure,' he said slowly, watching Alicia. He nodded at the others, smiled goodbye at Magda and followed Alicia out. As they reached the lobby, his fingers slid under her elbow with a biting grip, slowing her quick walk. They stepped outside into the sunlit street and he pulled her to a stop.

'Now, what was that all about?' he demanded. His eyes angrily took in Alicia's defiant face.

'What?' she inquired shortly.

'Don't play dumb.' His long, strong fingers tightened. 'What do you mean by giving me an ultimatum?'

'What did she say to you?' Alicia jerked out, not denying it.

'*Say?*' he quoted incredulously. 'Let me think: "Hello Devereaux, remember me, sorry to hear about your accident." That's about it. Why?'

'She was your mistress!' Alicia bit out fiercely.

Dev's face changed, his eyes narrowing. He drew her down the steps, across the pavement and put her without a word into the car parked along the kurb. He crossed round and got in beside Alicia.

'All right,' he said quietly, 'talk.'

Alicia looked briefly at his grim face. She said bitterly, 'There's nothing to say. She was your mistress—'

'When?' he interrupted.

'Before we were married.' She cut off the end of her thought, 'and maybe after.'

'So?' he snapped.

'*So*.' Her voice broke.

'Yes! So what? I don't even remember her, for God's sake!'

'She remembers you.'

Dev stared at her and then half turned, looking unseeingly out the window. 'Terrific.'

Alicia bit her knuckle to keep herself from crying.

'There's more to it than that,' he said flatly, after a long dreary silence.

She shook her head.

'The hell there isn't!' he said, loosing the tight rein of his temper. 'You acted like—' He bit it off and said in a dangerous tone, 'You ever pull that mistress of the manor act again, lady, and you are in for a surprise.' He was silent for a moment, then said more quietly, 'This has to do with the other, doesn't it? With not wanting me to remember?'

She couldn't answer.

Dev raked his hand through his hair impatiently.

'What *is* it?' he pressed. 'What are you so afraid of my finding out?'

She shook her head without speaking.

'Alicia—' his voice grew gentle as he turned to her, 'talk to me.'

'What is so hard to understand about my not liking her?' Alicia blurted out, to divert his attention.

It was Dev's turn to remain silent.

'I'm jealous!' she grated.

'You've nothing to be jealous of.'

She gave a short, hysterical laugh. Dev's hand shot out, turning her face to his. 'All right, that's enough! Tell me what it is I've done.'

'Nothing,' Alicia got out. 'You wouldn't understand.'

'I sure as hell don't understand this!'

Alicia jerked her head away, found the car handle and opened the door. Dev caught her wrist with his hand, and she tried uselessly to jerk free, then said with an assumption of calm.

'I've got to drive my car home.'

He let her go and said warningly, 'We're going to talk this out—today.'

It was Mrs Larke's day off and the house felt empty, cool and silent. Dev walked into the sitting room and poured himself a drink. Alicia followed, pausing in the doorway.

'Would you like something?' he asked. He looked remote, his tilted eyes cool.

'No—thanks.' She clasped her arms around herself, waiting.

He continued to watch her, drinking. Alicia's nerves tightened like screws. With childish stubbornness she kept her mouth clamped shut, determined that he would not drag the information he sought out of her.

Dev continued to drink, apparently oblivious to any tension.

Was he angry? She began to wonder nervously what went on beneath the chiselled mask of his face. Why didn't he speak? He had said they would talk, now he stood, coolly drinking his drink and watching her as though he were critiquing a painting. Did he not care any more? Was he trying to wear down her defences?

'Well?' she demanded in an aggressive voice that echoed slightly in the still room.

'Well?' he returned politely.

'You said we'd talk.'

'I'm listening.'

Alicia shrugged. 'I don't know what you want to hear.'

'The truth would be nice.' He set the drink on the mantelpiece above the cold fireplace.

She shrugged again and pushed her hands into the pockets of her linen dress, walking a little further into the room. She hated feeling that she was behaving like a sulky child; that was how he was treating her; that was how she was acting.

'I shouldn't have been rude. I'm sorry,' she said abruptly.

'Okay.' He nodded, still biding his time.

'I'm jealous of her,' Alicia offered again.

'Why?'

'You know why!'

'No. So she was my mistress once. I married *you*.'

'But you don't love me!' It was out in one angry little sentence, revealing bottomless pain. She saw his eyes widen before she turned away, too humiliated to face him.

'What are you talking about?' he asked blankly. Of course I love you.'

'Of course I love you.'

The words reverberated in Alicia's empty brain like a stone crashing to the bottom of a cliff. She listened to the echo numbly, not believing. Once before he had told her he loved her. He had not meant what she meant by love.

'You're—*fond* of me,' she managed, in a reasonable tone.

Dev came up behind her, turning her to face him. She tried to smile, her eyes touching his briefly, then sliding away. He was frowning, his breath warm on her cheek.

'I love you,' he repeated carefully. He tilted her face up again for scrutiny, his green eyes puzzled.

She shook her head quickly, denying it.

'Yes, I do,' he argued gently. His lips feathered the corner of her quivering mouth. 'How could you think anything else?' he murmured and kissed her again, coaxingly.

'You—' Alicia cleared her throat. 'You're grateful—since your accident.'

Dev laughed. Her eyes raised disbelievingly.

'Grateful?' he said ironically. 'Because my wife stayed by me?'

'You've never said you loved me!' she objected.

'I say it every day.' He added after a reflective moment, 'Maybe not in those three words, but—surely you can tell?'

She hesitated. Yes, he did behave lovingly; but the memory of before kept her from accepting the face value of his actions.

'When we married,' Dev said slowly, 'I must have told you then I loved you?'

'But it's different now,' Alicia said quickly. She didn't want him pursuing that train of thought. 'As far as you know we began from the first time I came to see you in the hospital.'

He accepted that. 'All right, then I fell in love with you all over again. But you must have realised that?'

He grinned faintly. 'You don't honestly think it's out of *gratitude* that I can't keep my hands off you?'

He was always touching her, holding her, caresses out of erotic context. But she said rationally, 'It could just be sex.'

'It could be a lot more than that. It's everything, from the way you look sleeping to the way your mind jumps around, thought to thought, like a little frog. I can't explain it. I just need to have you with me. Things are better when you're here.' He smiled at her, his eyes tender and steady, amused that she didn't know how it was with him.

Alicia couldn't believe she was hearing this. She stared up at him and Dev said with slight impatience, 'I wish there were better, newer words to explain how I feel. It sounds so trite, so hackneyed—' His face changed with an idea, before Alicia could tell him he was doing just fine.

'Look—' He turned her, drawing Alicia out of the room and up the stairs. She wondered for a moment exactly what he had in mind, but somewhat to her disappointment he dragged her past their bedroom, down the hallway to the studio.

He pulled her into the room, guiding her forward and pointing to the freshly completed portrait of herself. He must have finished it and come to the Gallery to take her to lunch.

'What does that tell you?' he queried, putting his hands on his lean hips.

Alicia stared at the portrait, conscious of his eyes on her. He had painted her framed in the window seat, sitting legs crossed, Indian-style. She wore a floppy straw hat, her chin was propped on her hand, her profile three-quarters turned. It was a rather childish pose, yet she did not look like a child in the simple, white peasant-style dress. Her body looked slender and brown, but subtly sensual. Her profile was as pure as a child's, but her eyes had a warm, knowledgeable smile, her lips curved with humorous invitation.

She glanced at Dev's watchful expression, then back at the portrait. The precocious child quality of the former portraits was absent. She looked like a woman, young, open, sensitive, but mature. And loved. From the dusty gold tangle of her hair beneath the broad-brimmed hat, to the peep of brown toes below the layered white skirt, the woman in the portrait looked loved.

'I don't know what to say,' she whispered slowly, turning to her husband.

Dev quirked an eyebrow. 'How about, "ah yes, I see what you mean"? And how about, "I love you, too"?'

For the first time in what seemed like days, Alicia felt like laughing. She put her hands out, tentatively, slipping them over his shoulders, locking them behind his head. His hair felt crisply soft to her touch, as his head bent. His lips touched hers, firm and cool, once, twice, a third time. Alicia melted against his hard strength, her heart beginning to slam against her ribs.

'After all,' Dev murmured, 'I'm not the one who goes on picking up strangers in art galleries.' Then his mouth moved urgently. Alicia was aware of a fierce hunger to equal his as all humour died within her. She loved him so much. She wanted him so much—and there was no reason not to. He loved her. She could feel it in the tension of his lean virile body, in the thundering heart beneath her ear, in the faint unsteadiness of his hands as they touched her, moved her. She need never hesitate or regret again. Alicia abandoned herself to Dev's seeking mouth and demanding hands, all thought swept aside and lost, like blossoms caught in an eddy . . .

Usually the days seemed to fly by at the Gallery, but today lingered endlessly. Alicia stared down the long, chilly, white hallway, lined with paintings, and felt like someone trapped in a science fiction movie. By day she was a museum piece, by night a live woman. It was a slow day, the Gallery nearly empty, perhaps that was it. By closing time, Alicia felt she had waited a lifetime.

Whereas yesterday's drive had seemed unnervingly brief, today's appeared endless. The road seemed to have an elastic quality; home stretched further and further out of reach. Then the elastic snapped, and without warning, Alicia was home.

She went into the house, calling a cheerful greeting to Mrs Larke dusting the study, and set her bag on the hall table. Pudgy came scampering down the stairs to greet her, half tripping over her increasingly large paws.

'Well, hello there!' Alicia exclaimed, bending down, and Pudgy ecstatically banged into her, pink tongue licking frantically.

'Is Dev upstairs?' Alicia breathlessly asked Mrs Larke. Mrs Larke nodded, waving her duster like a traffic policeman.

Alicia rose and started up the staircase, Pudgy dodging at her feet, in an apparent effort to steal a shoe. Reaching the landing, the puppy scurried ahead, straight into the bedroom.

Alicia paused in her beeline for the studio, and followed Pudgy's wagging tail, pushing wide the bedroom door. She paused, her hand on the door-knob.

Dev was seated on the edge of the bed, unresponsive to Pudgy's wriggling, wagging bid for attention. He raised his head to meet Alicia's eyes, and his face was as white and rigid as marble. Alicia's eyes fell to the violet pool of silk on the coverlet beside him. Her breath caught, recognising the old Victorian gown she had worn for her first portrait. Until now it had hung, unremembered, in the back of her closet.

She knew, even before he said in a hard, expressionless voice, 'I've remembered—everything.'

Her legs felt weak and trembly, her mouth dry. 'Oh.'

No doubt he felt the inadequacy of that remark; he threw her a hostile look.

Alicia leaned back against the wall for support. 'Well,' she said breathlessly, 'does it matter?'

His expression was incredulous. 'So long as you get what you want? You've gone to pretty extreme lengths to keep up the farce, haven't you? I'd no idea appearances meant so much.'

'It wasn't like that,' she got out stiffly.

'No? Then you explain why you didn't want me to get my memory back. It couldn't be because this way you had exactly what you wanted, could it?'

'Yes, but what I wanted isn't what you think I wanted,' she cried confusedly. Pudgy looked from Dev to Alicia, whining at the unfamiliar loud, excited voices.

'Of course,' Dev said with a cynical smile, 'love.'

It was like a nightmare, Alicia thought hazily. His eyes were hard and bright, cutting like razors into her spirit. 'That's exactly what it was,' she said in a hopeless tone.

For some reason that seemed to make him angrier. He got up from the bed, going to where she stood limply propped by the wall, and towered menacingly.

'In your own way,' he bit out, 'you're as ruthless as the rest of us. Maybe it's rich-girl syndrome. You can't take no, can you? No effort is too great, no price too high to get what you want. You wanted a—what were the words again?—a loving, devoted husband, and you got one! Why don't you just admit it?'

'Because it's not true!' Alicia said fiercely. 'You know me better than that! I don't care what it looks like, I didn't lie because I couldn't stand admitting I'd been made a fool of! I lied because I loved you, and I was afraid that when your memory came back you would hate me.'

'Loved me?' he laughed shortly. 'You threw me out of here screaming you hated me. The same look was in your eyes that day in front of the flat.'

'I didn't realise till you were ill—' she broke off as he shook his head disbelievingly. 'What did you expect?' she cried. 'You had *humiliated* me. You made me a fool! Yes, I hated you, but hated you because I loved you!'

'So you tried your best to do the same to me?' he said bitterly.

'Why can't you understand?' she asked desperately, her hands touched his pleadingly. 'Nothing has changed. Not really. We've been happy together, up until now.'

'Our happiness was founded on lies,' he told her impatiently, shaking off her hands.

'It's founded on love,' Alicia argued.

Pudgy began to bark agitatedly.

'I can't *help* what happened in the past,' she said,

trying to speak calmly, over Pudgy. 'But it's insane to throw everything away because of a past we can't change!'

'You're right,' he said flatly, 'you can't change the past.'

They stared at each other.

'Which means what?' Alicia inquired unsteadily.

'Which means I've got to think.' He opened the door beside her and went out. Alicia heard his footsteps on the landing, Pudgy straggling curiously behind.

Alicia crossed slowly to the window. After a few moments had passed, she watched Dev come out of the house, cross the front court and climb into the Ferrari. She stared dully as he backed the car and pulled out of the court, vanishing down the shady drive.

CHAPTER ELEVEN

TRAILING over to the bed, Alicia sat down where Dev had sat, and touched the shabby silk dress with gentle fingers.

She wondered drearily, how he had come to find the dress. Pudgy probably. She was always digging in the closet for new and unusual shoes to chew. Alicia could imagine Dev reaching in to haul her out and spotting the dress, peeping between the other never-worns.

She sighed, a long shaky sigh. She wished she could cry, her throat throbbed painfully, her eyes burned. But she felt too numb, too empty. She could barely take it in. She had stopped believing he would recover his memory. She had trusted to luck. If she thought about it at all, she had reassured herself that if the moment ever came she could make him understand.

She realised the returning memory must have come as a shock—that final scene fresh in his mind as his last conscious thought. But he had other memories to weigh against it, memories of these past months. How could he dismiss everything they had shared? They were wasting time and energy on side issues. The only fact that really mattered was that they loved each other. She had learned that the hard way, why couldn't Dev realise it as well?

Perhaps he would. She clung to that hope like a shipwrecked sailor to a spar. Perhaps after he had time to think, to weigh the past against the present?

Dev didn't have an unforgiving nature. Nor did he lack insight. Surely when he had time to think?

Alicia continued to sit, her thoughts winding around and around in her head in a twisting circle. She listened absently for the Ferrari, watching Pudgy gnaw contentedly on her favourite shoe.

Gradually she began to get mad. She was sitting here, praying that Dev would forgive her—and why? Wasn't it all his fault to begin with? Wasn't he the one who had originally misled and used *her*? Hadn't everything she had done been reaction to what *he* had done?

Alicia's anger seeped away, minute by minute. She tried to whip it up, reminding herself of her humiliation. Nothing worked. What was the point, anyway? She still loved him. Any harm he had done had been unintentional.

The room grew shadowy and dark. Pudgy fell asleep on the floor, her little round sides rising and falling gently.

Mrs Larke came up to say goodbye for the day.

'Mr Rafferty said you would be eating out tonight,' she said, her eyes curious on Alicia's figure at the window. The room was dusky, Alicia had not put on any lights.

'Yes,' Alicia said without turning.

'Goodnight, then.' Mrs Larke sounded hesitant.

'Goodnight.'

The house felt emptier than ever when the sounds of Mrs Larke's car died away. It was dark and still; lonely. Alicia continued to stare out of the window as though she could make Dev's headlights appear by will.

In the gloom she heard Pudgy yawn. Moments later a warm, small body clambered over her feet, demanding attention. Alicia bent, scooping the pup-py up and cradled it against her, rubbing her cheek against the silky head. A warm, eager tongue licked at her face and ear.

He might never come back. She hadn't allowed herself to consider that until now. It didn't seem possible, feeling as she did about him. But Dev was different. He had spent a lifetime happily self-sufficient. Emotionally he was cooler, detached. Maybe he had decided she didn't matter that much. Maybe he had had enough of domesticity. Maybe he just wouldn't come home.

Pudgy licked zealously at the hot, salty tears slowly sliding down Alicia's cheeks to the puppy's soft fur.

It was very late when she heard his car. Alicia had been lying there, not sleeping for hours. She hear the Ferrari's grumbling purr, like a giant, sulky cat in the court below. Seconds later she heard the car door slam. Her heart began to thud.

She rolled over, her feet dislodging Pudgy curled in a ball at the foot of the bed, and looked at the luminous dial of the clock: one in the morning. Pudgy half fell, half jumped from the bed, padding across to her basket. She settled in with a squeaky yawn, audible clear across the room.

Alicia listened to the front door bang, then to his quiet, slow footsteps on the stairs. She twisted over, burying her face in her pillow. Her nerves couldn't take it. She was ready to scream with tension.

She heard him in the doorway and looked up. He was a dark shadow moving in the gloom, approaching the bed.

'I'm awake,' she said. 'You can turn on the light.'

But he sat down on his side of the bed, without reaching to the lamp. Alicia raised herself on her elbow, staring at his obscure bulk. He smelt of the night, cold and sharply damp, like moonlit grass. Her nostrils quivered.

'Where were you?' She was careful to keep any kind of critical inflection from her voice.

'Driving. Walking.' He used the same neutral tone.

'You should have told me,' he said finally. It sounded like something he had been repeating to himself over and over.

'I couldn't at first.' She wanted to explain this properly. There wasn't room for any more misunderstandings. 'How could I, when you were ill? And then later, I didn't want to ruin—' She stopped and took a deep breath. 'I was hoping that you would fall in love with me—for real. That was the only way I knew to erase the past.'

'You can't erase the past.'

Alicia fought a wave of depression at his words. 'All right, but you can—neutralise it. That's what I wanted to do, make it not matter any more.'

'I don't see how my falling in love with you again could accomplish that.' There was a quality in his tone that frightened her. It was too lacking in feeling. He was standing back from her emotionally. She sensed that he had already played this scene out in his head, and reached his own conclusions. He was going through the motions, but he didn't feel it.

'Because,' she asserted, 'if you fell in love with me I knew it would be for myself. I could forget the past.'

'I was in love with you before we separated. You knew that. I told you.' He sounded cold, a little solid, healthy anger creeping back, against his efforts.

'I know,' she said simply. 'I didn't believe it then. Dev, you don't know what it was like for me. It practically killed me to think that you married me because of pity!'

'And money,' he said caustically, 'don't let's forget that.'

'And the money,' she agreed steadily. 'But I adored you.'

'Who asked you to!' he said, suddenly fierce, turning to her. 'Who asked you to come along with those big blue eyes and that girlish hero-worship! I told you—my God, you weren't *that* naïve! You knew—that was part of what you admired so much, if you'd admit it to yourself. And I've had to pay for it. You stripped me of everything, right down to my bloody self-respect!'

They were both silent, listening to the bitterness of that. Then he sighed and said wearily. 'I'm a man and not a particularly good one. What did you think would happen? You offered me—oh hell! You offered a fortune and yourself besides. I took it.'

After a long pause, he said almost sadly, 'I didn't see it as I do now. I honestly thought it was in your interests as well.'

'Did you care about me—really?' Alicia questioned softly.

He gave a rather cynical laugh. 'I know it's hard to believe, but I wouldn't have touched ten times your money, if I hadn't. You were the—neatest kid. So unspoilt.' He shrugged a little. 'Before I knew it I was in love with you—for the first time in my life.' He laughed with short, biting scorn.

'I understand all that now,' Alicia offered. 'I've grown up a lot. When it first happened I couldn't handle it. It made me bitter and cynical about everyone, including myself. I didn't believe that you had learned to love me. I didn't see how you could; I had no confidence left. I hated you for doing that to me.'

He listened to her without replying.

'I hadn't any experience to fall back on, and I hadn't anyone to talk to,' Alicia ran on urgently. 'I didn't know what to do, I hated you but—I still loved you, too. That was why I went to your flat and said all that stuff about a marriage on my terms. I didn't know how else to get you back.'

She swallowed nervously at his stillness.

'When you were hurt, I was glad. I mean, I could get you back and save face, and maybe you would fall in love with me—the new me. I know I should have told you,' she added pleadingly, 'but I couldn't! It was my only chance to find out if you could really love me. Can't you understand that?'

'Can't you understand that, under the circumstances, your keeping quiet was *intolerable*?' he demanded quietly. 'I've been living on your money for months—under these circumstances can't you see how—' he groped for a word '—insulting and unforgivable that was? Don't you think I have any pride?'

'You didn't mind before,' Alicia protested bewilderedly.

'When? I never took your money—'

'No, these past months since your illness.'

'I figured we had reached some decision about it before my accident.'

'Yes, because you trusted yourself not to have accepted any arrangement you didn't feel was respectable. And besides, don't you see how silly this is? You married me for my money then refused to touch it? Dev, *I'm* not worried about the money aspect any more! I think I always knew it wasn't just the money. If it was just money you were after you could have it any time, by painting portraits for Jacqueline's crowd. But you hold out. You have artistic integrity. And you have personal integrity.'

'The two aren't synonymous,' he said bitterly.

'Dev, you know you have personal integrity,' she tried to say chidingly.

He didn't reply, and she said drearily, 'But maybe what you're trying to say is you can't forgive *me*.'

That got his attention. 'Forgive you for what?' he asked blankly.

'Rich-girl syndrome? You said it yourself just a moment ago. I held out on the truth and I hired that detective. I didn't care if keeping you ignorant about us would hurt you.'

'Oh, don't be silly,' he said crisply.

'I've killed your love, haven't I?' Alicia said dully, ignoring him. 'Just like before.'

'What are you talking about, just like before?' The bed creaked under him as he turned towards her. His breath was cool and light against her face.

'When I sent you away, and said those awful things, you didn't try to explain or argue. You just left. You didn't try to contact me—'

'How could I?' he inquired. 'You hated me. I hated myself. There was nothing I could say to change your mind; it was all true. I told you I loved you; you didn't want to hear it. So I cleared out. That was what you seemed to want.'

'But if you cared—'

'I did care!' he said tautly. 'It was sheer hell, those weeks! I couldn't sleep or eat, I couldn't concentrate on my work. There was no point to anything I did. I had to face the fact that I loved you—and I had killed your love for me. You're the only person I've ever known who . . . trusted me, looked up to me—' he broke off huskily. 'I wanted to be what you thought I was—oh damn! What's the use!'

'The day I went to your apartment, to ask you to come back, you looked at *me* with hate,' she said.

He gave another sharp disbelieving laugh. 'It wasn't exactly like that,' he commented drily. 'You didn't exactly ask me to come back. You . . . said . . . things—' He seemed to have difficulty getting that out. After an electric silence, he said flatly, steadily, 'I hated myself, not you. I was mad as hell at you, but I've never hated you.'

She held her breath, praying. For a moment she thought it was over, that he was going to reach out to her, but instead he got off the bed. It creaked, echoing her protest. He went to the window, his form sharply illuminated against the starry sky outside. He put his hands in his pocket and tilted his head back as though his neck were stiff.

'I've thought it over and over. You're everything I'm not,' he said clearly, crisply. 'You're honest and innocent and sweet and serene. You've got all your lovely illusions intact—despite the bashing I gave them.' He gave a brief laugh. 'I'd like to think that if I were about ten years younger, it would be different, but at your age I was already too far gone.'

He sighed, 'Which leaves us where?' and rubbed the back of his neck with his hand.

Alicia scrambled out of bed, crossing the cold, carpeted floor to his side. She peered up at his remote face. 'Talk about lovely illusions intact!' she ejaculated. 'Since when did I become a saint? If you want

out of this marriage you'll have to find a better
excuse than that!'

He looked down, his eyes colourless and gleaming
in the dim light. He smiled faintly at her tone.

'So we're different?' Alicia stated. 'Isn't that the
whole point? That we balance each other? I've
known lots of nice uncomplicated boys. They bored
me to death. You said it yourself, it's your—' she
paused, searching for a word.

'Yes?' he queried drily.

'I don't know what it is,' she finished vaguely. 'But
it's exciting. And even if I were a saint, one saint in
the family is enough. You don't even ask whether
we've been happy together—'

'Have you been happy?' he asked, trying to read
her face. 'Considering everything, can you honestly
say you've been happy?'

'Don't you *know*?' Alicia whispered. 'Yesterday
you gave me everything. Today you want to take it all
back.'

'Alicia—' he stopped almost helplessly.

'Dev,' she murmured, lifting her face to his, 'why
are you looking for problems when there aren't any?'

'Nothing is that simple,' he muttered.

'No, it's this simple,' she half chuckled, and
touched her lips to his in a little persuasive kiss.
'Why do you want to go on punishing yourself—and
me? The past is past.' She kissed him again.

Dev's arms fastened around her, clamping her to
him. His lips moved with answering hunger under
Alicia's.

When he released her, she leaned against him
weakly.

'Oh, Dev,' she whispered.

'Oh, Alicia,' he mocked gently, resting her head

against his hair and cradling her tightly against him. 'You're getting the short end of the stick here, but I've been about as noble as I can be for as long as I can stand.' He kissed the bridge of her nose lightly.

'Thank God,' she said fervent with relief. She laughed suddenly.

'Mm?' Dev whispered, kissing her ear. His arms felt warm and strong and loving about her. Heart's haven, she thought contentedly, remembering what he had once said to her.

'I was just thinking,' she chuckled in answer to his inquiry, 'if only Aunt Elizabeth knew: this is one time the heiress bags the fortune-hunter!'